MW01681121

A LEGAL BRIEFS NOVELLA
Book Two

Next of Kin

MARIE SINCLAIR

Next of Kin

Published by Sinbooks Ink: www.sinbinbooks.com

contact: marie.sinbooks@gmail.com

Digital eBook ISBN: 978-1-958257-31-9

Paperback ISBN: 978-1-958257-32-6

About Next of Kin

Nick

I've always been the playboy of my friend group. The guy who's never been without a boyfriend or girlfriend or at least a regular hookup since high school. But lately, casual isn't doing it for me. It's a fact that becomes abundantly clear when I can't get it up for a hot guy I met at a coffeeshop and invited back to my place. He's gracious and leaves without making it a big deal. Even offers me a raincheck if I want. Which I don't. When I hear the police sirens about a half hour after he left, I don't think anything of it except to wonder if they can find my missing libido.

Aaron

After my brother, Zack, is found in an alley, everything becomes about finding his killer. Unfortunately, neither the police nor my family have any idea what Zack was doing in that part of San Francisco. I mean, I have a suspicion, but with Zack's phone missing, the police don't know where to look. At a loss about what to do but needing to do something, Zack's best friend and I start handing out flyers trying to find someone who saw Zack or knew where he'd been. It's a long shot, but miraculously, someone calls to say he might have been the last person to see Zack alive.

Meeting under the most unlikeliest of circumstances, Nick and Aaron find a connection neither of them anticipated. A connection that leads them into each others arms and each others hearts.

Trigger Warnings: death of a sibling, grief, and addiction, (off page) acts of violence.

Contents

One

NICK

OF COURSE, THE GUY pauses at my door instead of leaving because what would make my humiliation more complete than the pity in his expression? Hint: nothing. Except…

"It's no big deal," the guy says, and I cringe knowing the next words out of his mouth are going to be…yep, "It happens to all of us."

Yeah. While that might be true for other guys, it has *NEVER* happened to me before, and I can't get this guy out of my apartment fast enough so I can forget about the utter mortification of watching my erection shrivel and die while a hot guy was begging me to destroy him.

"Ping me if you want to meet up again," he says, and *dear God, can't he just go?*

"I'll keep that in mind," I say doing my best not to shove him into the hallway so I can close the door and forget this ever happened.

He leans in as if he's going to kiss me but stops at the last minute and gives me a smile which at least makes my lifeless dick twitch. Too little, too late. I am not going to invite this guy back inside and risk a repeat performance of my failure to achieve liftoff.

"I'll see you around," he says before he turns toward the elevator and gets out of my life.

I do my best to close the door quietly behind him. It would be rude to slam it because the whole debacle is not his fault. I'm the one who couldn't get it up. Fuck. My. Life. Seriously, this has never happened to me before, and I'm not handling it well. At. All.

My brain is helpfully stuck on an endless repeat of the whole embarrassing evening. Everything plays through my mind from seeing the guy's profile on Grindr while waiting for my coffee at Spike's and discovering he was right around the corner at Philz doing the same thing, to the quick texts giving him directions to where I'd parked my car, the tension humming between us as I'd driven home. We'd barely made it through the front door before our tongues were in each other's mouths. He was gorgeous and willing and my dick had been totally on board with the whole thing up until I opened the condom.

I'd laughed about it, suggested a glass of wine might help. We'd made out a bit in between sips, slowly working ourselves back up to our previous frenzy, my cock gallantly rising to the occasion as I bent the guy over the back of my couch.

"Oh, yeah, fucking destroy my ass," he'd moaned. "Tear me up and make me beg."

And that was all it took for my hard-on to wither and die, leaving me mortified. In my embarrassment, I probably acted like a jerk trying to get the guy out of my place as quickly as I could, but I was having a difficult time dealing with what had happened.

Twice. It had happened twice.

I return to my living room and gather the two half-full wine glasses from the coffee table and take them into the kitchen. I don't bother straightening the cushions on the couch or picking up my shirt or the limp condom and empty wrapper from the floor.

What. The. Fuck?

I snort as I open the fridge, take out a beer and return to the living room to wallow in my disgrace. With a frown at the detritus of my failed evening, I flop onto the couch and take a long pull of the beer.

Destroy me.

I don't get it. I really don't. All the pieces were there. The guy—yeah, I can't remember his name, I'll add it to the list of reasons I'm an asshole—was hot, horny, and here. Those are the three things that have mattered most to me since I was fourteen and discovered I liked boys as much as I liked girls. My friends tease me that I haven't gone a week without sex since my sixteenth birthday and take bets on how quickly I'll find someone new after a breakup. I'm our group's resident slut, the one who always has a boyfriend or girlfriend or a steady fuck buddy or easily scores hookups whenever I find myself without any of those.

And, not once in the twenty-five years of my existence, has my dick failed to rise to the occasion.

It happens to all of us.

Well, not me, my man. Not. Fucking. Me.

I take another pull on the beer, pick up the TV remote and scroll through the apps in search of something to take my mind off the situation. Right after the opening credits of a stupid cop movie I've watched more times than I'd like to admit, my phone buzzes with a text from my friend Tyler.

Cam and I are heading to Breaux tonight. Want to join us?

Making a face at my phone because yes, what would be a more perfect end to my evening than hanging out with my insanely happy friend and the guy he met while on jury duty last year.

Sorry. Can't. Busy, I type back.

Ty sends me back the rolling eye emoji, and I send him back an eggplant and a peach.

Be safe, my friend, Ty texts.

Always am, I respond, which gets me a heart sticker but no more texts.

I stare at my phone wondering if I shouldn't get into my club clothes and go out with them. And then I remember that my dick isn't working tonight and focus my attention on the movie. What's the point of going out when I had a gorgeous guy beneath me less than half an hour ago and couldn't close the deal? I don't need another reminder of my failure.

I'm in the kitchen getting another beer when I hear the sirens. At first, I think the sounds are from the TV, but then I see the blue and red lights reflecting off the walls as a police car passes my building. It's not a common occurrence in this neighborhood—Hayes Valley is fairly upscale—but San Francisco is a city and things happen. I hope it's something minor like a fender bender and that no one's hurt, then wonder if those police officers could help me find my missing libido.

Two

Aaron

THE PAST TWO WEEKS have been a shit show. There's no other way to describe what's happened to my family since the police called and asked my folks to identify Zack's body. *That* was a full twenty-four hours *after* my parents attempted to report him missing and got blown off because, and I quote, "Zack is an adult who is in his rights to not answer his phone or be at home. He can go on vacation, and not text, call, or contact anyone in your family or any of his friends to let them know."

No matter how much we insisted it was completely out of character for him to do any of that, the police refused to open a case. And then it turned out they'd found him dead in an alley the night before my parents contacted the police because Zack hadn't shown up to our family brunch. The police had been unable to identify him immediately because his wallet and phone had been taken, and my brother's fingerprints weren't in any of their databases. It was only because of my parents' insistence that the police finally took a report which then linked to the John Doe they were trying to identify.

My parents are numb with grief, and my sister consumed with taking care of them while also assisting the police in their investigation, so arranging Zack's funeral fell to me. The details had kept me blissfully distracted, my mind focused on making it a celebration of his twenty-eight years on this planet, but my mother's near-constant tears and questions about why and how this happened to her baby had been a steady reminder that we weren't going to find closure until we had answers.

After the funeral, when it had just been me, my sister and parents, and a few of Zack's closest friends, someone finally asked the question none of us had been able to answer. "What the hell was he doing in Hayes Valley? He hated that neighborhood."

I have a suspicion, but it wasn't one I was going to voice in front of my parents. It wasn't that they didn't know Zack was gay or had an issue with it for either him or me, it was that they didn't know Zack liked anonymous sex with men he met on Grindr and Scruff. My younger brother may have been an absolute day trading genius, but the risks he took with money were only surpassed by those he took with his body, and his stories of inviting men he didn't know into his home had left me worried for his safety more times than I cared to think about. There was no way my mother needed to know these things now that he was gone.

It's not that I'm judgmental about the choices Zack made. I'd unsuccessfully used those apps myself a few times, but the apps were *all* Zack did to meet guys for one-offs. He'd had a few dodgy hookups that resulted in bruises he didn't ask for and a couple of close calls with gaybaiting assholes. I'd offered to go out to clubs with him more than a few times, but my brother was an adrenaline junkie through and through. He liked the danger, the uncertainty, the rush. And, he'd assured me, ninety-nine percent of his hookups turned out to be fine. I hated to think this one hadn't.

As one week turned into two, the police were getting nowhere very fast. There had been no witnesses, just the waiter who'd found my brother's body when he stepped into the alley to have a smoke on his break. None of the cameras that might have picked up what happened had been working that night, and a canvass of the area hadn't turned up anyone who'd seen or heard a thing. No one remembered seeing Zack at any of the restaurants or bars that evening. His credit cards didn't show payments to Hayes Valley shops or receipts to any of the ride share apps. Without his phone, it was impossible to know what he'd been doing or where he'd been until the police could get his phone records, but I knew that wouldn't help us if he'd hooked up with someone from an app. Everyone knew Zack's murder was turning ice cold, which meant no answers for my parents.

We've got to do something.

The text comes from Zack's best friend, Kit, on the two-week anniversary of Zack's murder. I agree with him, but I've got no idea what to do.

Maybe we should go to Hayes Valley tonight to see if we can find someone who saw Zack that night, Kit suggests.

The police have already tried. No one saw him.

My phone buzzes with an incoming call from Kit.

"I can't stand this," he says as soon as I accept the call.

"I know."

"God, Aaron, how can you be so...I don't know...complacent about this?"

"You think I'm fucking complacent? Jesus Christ, Kit. He was my brother. My mom's barely keeping it together, my dad's near catatonic at his best moments, and Shayna's running herself ragged between taking care of them and her kids. I'm on the phone with the police every fucking day, but they can't do anything without a lead, and they've got nothing."

Kit grumbles at me, but I know he knows this. We've been through it so many times. What was Zack doing in Hayes Valley? Where had he been earlier in the day? What had we missed?

"I keep thinking," Kit says. "We were supposed to get together, but I got caught by a deadline at work, so I had to cancel at the last minute."

I know where he's going with this. "It's not your fault," I say.

"Yeah. In my head I know that, but the thought's there. If only..."

But something in what Kit says makes me think. "He was working all day," I say. "So, he was at home." I picture my brother hunched over his computer analyzing numbers and following the rise and fall of what he called 'financial instruments,' about which I still had no clue despite Zack's attempts to explain it and get me to join him and his day trading friends. Unlike my brother, I'm not a risk taker, and my job as a logistics coordinator for a biomed firm suits me just fine.

"Where were you guys going to meet?" I ask Kit, small bits of information turning in my head as I try to fit them into a larger picture.

"Philz on Market in the Castro."

"It's possible he met someone around there," I say.

"Yeah. Maybe."

We both fall silent, and I picture my brother getting Kit's text while standing in line, then getting on an app to find a hookup now that his evening was free. "That was his regular coffee place, wasn't it?" I ask. "It's only a couple of blocks from his apartment."

Kit agrees with me. "He'd go there when he needed to get out of the house."

"Think they'd remember seeing him?" I ask, a plan already formulating.

"It's worth a try. Hell, anything's better than waiting for the police to do more of this nothing."

And that's how I end up outside the Philz in the Castro asking people to take a look at a photo of my brother and asking if they remembered seeing him two weeks before.

Three

Nick

"So, what's the latest body count?" Avy asks as soon as I sit down at the table with my friends.

I roll my eyes and look around for the waiter so I can order a drink. These are the people I'm closest to, the ones I've known since elementary school and who know me best. Most of the time, it's great that we've stayed so close, getting together as a whole group at least once or twice a month. Having people who share my history, who know who I am and all my stories is fantastic, but sometimes it feels like I'm stuck in the role I filled as a teenager, and they won't ever see me any other way.

Not that I usually mind because it's true more often than not, and I can be counted on to share enough details of my escapades to let the more pedestrian members of our group live vicariously. But not tonight. It's been two weeks since my disastrous failure, and I still can't shake the sting of it or the fear it will happen again. My last regular fuck buddy went and fell in love with his housemate about a year ago, and then there was a total trainwreck of a relationship that ended with my ex in handcuffs because her idea of breaking up was to trash my car. So, I've been finding people through the apps. Only, I haven't been able to bring myself to hook up with anyone just in case I have the same issue I had before.

Avy nudges my shoulder and raises an eyebrow at me. I sigh and give him what he wants.

"Still impressive," I say. "And getting bigger."

It's the first time in my life I've lied to my friends about my sex life, but Avy high fives me and says, "Of course, it is."

Thankfully, the waiter shows up so I can order the first of what I know will be several beers.

Talk goes on around me, but I'm only half-listening. Ty and Cam are, of course, sitting so close together at the other end of the table they might as well be the same person. We're waiting for them to announce their engagement any day now. Min tried to organize a betting pool for when we think it'll happen, but every one of us chose Valentine's Day because that will be Ty and Cam's one-year anniversary, so Min gave up. I mean, it has to be, right? They've got the best meet-cute story, having ended up seated next to each other for jury duty on a trial that ended on, you guessed it, Valentine's Day. From the night we all met Cam, it was obvious Ty was head-over-heels for him, and that was before they'd even gotten to know each other.

I figure we'll all get the ring pic from Ty in a few months when the hearts and flowers day rolls around again. Knowing the two of them, it's going to be one of those adorably cute proposals I've seen on Insta where they both try to surprise each other with rings and wind up pulling them out at the same time, then crying and hugging and telling each other how perfect they are for one another before professing their undying love and saying how happy they are.

Roman slides into the seat next to mine and unwinds the scarf from around their neck before shrugging out of their jacket. "How's it going?" they ask, and I tell them that it's the same old, same old.

"Work, fuck, sleep, and eat," they say and nod in understanding. It's my own mantra coming back at me from Roman's mouth.

"The four main food groups of a balanced life," I say, and we both laugh.

Despite being the quietest of our group and a direct contrast with myself in terms of relationships and sex—I don't think Roman's ever even dated—Roman is the friend I'm closest to in our group, someone I call my bestie because they've always gotten me in ways the others don't. Case in point...

"You doing okay, man? You seem a bit...off." Roman's dark eyes meet mine, and their brows crease a little. I'd tell them in a heartbeat what happened, but I honestly don't know how Roman would react. They came out as nonbinary in our senior year of high school, something that surprised no one in our friend group, and have said a few things since then that lead me to believe Roman is ace as well. So, while Roman might be sympathetic, it's not the same thing as being able to walk a mile in my shoes. Honestly, I don't know if there's anyone in this group to whom I could confide my failure.

"Yeah. Doing fine," I say with a shrug. "Just a little stressed at work."

"I hear that. Christmas shopping has already begun." Roman owns a bookstore in the Castro. As much as IT can be a nightmare of dealing with people who don't understand computers—seriously, how can someone not know you have to plug a computer in? They run on electricity!—some of the stories Roman tells about entitled, asshole customers make me thankful I don't work in retail.

Roman signals to the waiter and orders a vodka rocks when he comes over. I ask for another beer, and we settle in for our friend evening. Conversation flows freely between us all, side discussions forming between various members of the group—Min and Avy are the worst offenders, especially when they're seated next to each other—before returning to the topic at hand.

As we're tucking into our entrees, Min turns to me and asks if I know anything about the guy who'd gotten murdered a block from my building about two weeks before.

I shake my head as someone asks what happened.

Min shrugs her shoulders. "Don't know. There was just a guy handing out flyers near Philz in the Castro asking if anyone had seen his brother the afternoon of the twelfth, said it happened in Hayes Valley. I looked it up on my phone after, and all I could find was that someone had gotten killed in the alley. From what the guy said, it doesn't seem like the police have a lot to go on, so the family's trying to find anyone who might have witnessed something."

Murmurs of "how horrible" float around the table, and I nod in agreement even as I'm remembering the sirens and flashing lights the night of my embarrassing performance issues. Am I an asshole for finding a tiny bit of comfort in knowing that someone had a worse night than I had? Probably. But, as quickly as the thought surfaces, I push it away because my issue is irrelevant alongside what this guy's friends and family must be going through.

A FEW DAYS LATER, I'm meeting Ty for coffee so we can go over some stuff for his webcomic. Ty's been drawing shit since we were kids, turning all our adventures into comic strips and storylines and making up fantastic worlds and creatures. He's insanely talented and the way his webcomic *Undercover Ops* has been blowing up lately, he's not going to have to keep working as a graphic designer for much longer.

As our friend group's resident IT guy, I'm only too happy to help him whenever he's got a technical or computer issue to figure out. It's already earned me a recurring minor character in Ty's current storyline and a signed print of Cypher X, the character Ty drew for me, which I promptly framed and hung in my bedroom because who wouldn't want to be a badass and built special ops guy with mad hacking skills?

Since Ty moved in with Cam, he lives within walking distance of my neighborhood, so we're meeting at Loquat because he cannot get enough of their salted chocolate babka. I don't begrudge him because it means I can indulge in the pine nut and bay leaf tart along with some of the best coffee in the city, in my humble opinion.

I get there early so I can grab a good table, then order my coffee and open up my laptop to answer emails until Ty gets there about ten minutes later. He stops by the counter to place his order, then joins me at the back corner table.

"Nice spot," he says as he slides his messenger bag off his shoulder. His cheeks are pink from walking in the brisk morning air, but I know the sparkle in his eyes can only come from Cam.

"You look happy," I say as he sits next to me. "Wake up on the right side of the bed?"

Ty's cold-blushed cheeks turn a darker color, and he bites his lower lip as he ducks his head. "I always do," he says, but there's no tease in his voice, no smugness. He's dead-set serious, and I feel a tiny stab of envy that Ty's the first of us to find what looks like a permanent thing.

If I'd had to place a bet, I would have chosen Dan to be the first. He had a girlfriend all through senior year in high school and another his sophomore and junior year in college. I don't think he's ever had a hookup. The question is out of my mouth before I can think, and Ty flushes all over again, but this time he shakes his head at me.

"Jeez, Nick, is that all you ever think about?" The server places Ty's order on the table in front of him, and Ty takes a moment to savor his first sip of coffee. "And, for the record, I don't think so, but it's not something we discuss that often."

"But, you do discuss it." I wink at him. Teasing Ty has always been one of my favorite things to do because he gets flustered so easily.

"You're a pain in the ass."

"Most of the time," I say and laugh when Ty sputters on his next sip of coffee.

"Asshole."

I hold out my hands in surrender. "You're making this too easy, but please note the restraint I'm showing."

"Noted."

"And, for the record, hookups are not the only thing I ever think about."

Ty fixes me with his big, blue eyes. "You haven't told us about any dates lately," he says. "Are you having a dry spell?"

Unlike the way Avy had asked me about my love life at dinner, Ty's not trying to make a joke about it or get the juicy details about my latest conquest. Ty and I have a bond that was forged the day he joined Mr. Knowles' second grade class halfway through the school year. I'd been the new kid a few months earlier thanks to my parents' divorce and could tell how scared and unsure he was, so I volunteered to show him around and then introduced him to Roman and Dan at lunch.

Ty was our catalyst, our storyteller and master of games, always coming up with what we should play during recess. It rarely involved playground equipment or a ball, so other kids gravitated to us. By the end of the year, our group had grown to include Min, Avy, and Sasha, making us what we are now.

Sometimes, Ty got shit from teachers because he was always scribbling something instead of paying attention, but when he won a national writing award at the end of freshman year, he became the golden boy. Not that any of us begrudged him. Ty's talent is incredible, and he's always been there when any of us need him. I hope Cam knows how lucky he is to have Ty in his life.

"I mean, I know it's not any of my business," Ty says because he must see my 'oh shit' face in response to his dry spell question. "You don't have to answer that question if you don't want to."

"It's fine," I say with a shrug. "Honestly, I haven't been looking lately." Staring at the wall across from our table and the artwork by a local artist hopefully priced at seven hundred and fifty dollars a painting, I try to summon the courage to say the thing that's really on my mind.

"Is this because of that last chick? What was her name? The one that went after your car with a tire iron."

I shudder and shake my head. "That was Lauren." She's the ex who ended up in jail for destroying my car. "And no, I don't think this is because of her." Although...no, it wasn't because of her per se...but something niggles at me about that particular relationship. I just can't put my finger on what's got me feeling like the word I'm looking for isn't coming to mind, but I do know the most current issue is not because of her.

"Then what's going on?"

Leaning in, I motion Ty closer. "Can you keep something between us?" I ask.

"Of course. You know you don't even have to ask."

"Thanks. But seriously, this doesn't go anywhere else."

"Jesus, Nick, now I'm worried. Are you sick or something?"

"Not at all. Healthy as a horse. Except..." I take a deep breath, then lower my voice to make sure no one can overhear me. Ty leans in a bit more. "I had a guy a couple of weeks ago. Really hot. Totally into it. Only..." My gaze darts around the coffee shop then lands back on Ty's face.

"Only..." he prompts.

"...I couldn't get it up." My face burns with shame, and I desperately want to grab the words back, but they're out there now. To Ty's credit, he doesn't laugh, he doesn't tell me it happens to all guys at some point, and he doesn't look at me with pity in his expression. Thank fuck.

Ty nods, but I can tell he's struggling to figure out what to say to me, so I let him off the hook with a shrug and a lopsided smile. "Had to happen sometime, right?" I say. "Odds were against me with as much as I use it, you know?" Fuck. Now I'm making stupid jokes to try and get Ty to say something.

"Ye...ah," Ty responds slowly. "But I can tell it's really messed with your head."

"It has. Both of them, actually."

Ty sputters, then we both laugh and the tense moment passes.

"You're sure you're all right?" Ty asks. "I mean, physically. There could be a medical issue."

"I'm fine," I say, but when I see Ty gearing up to tell me to be a responsible adult, I cut him off. "I promise, if the problem persists, I'll go see my doctor. At the moment, the only thing that's damaged is my pride."

"Maybe," Ty says thoughtfully. "Or maybe you're tired of meaningless hookups and relationships that don't go anywhere."I wrinkle my nose at him. "Not everyone wants a ring and a white picket fence, Mr. Happily Ever After."

From the way Tyler blushes, I have to wonder if the rings are coming sooner than any of us thought. Christmas is less than a month away. Maybe I should have a word with Min about her stupid engagement pool.

With only a little more cajoling, we move on to discussing the issues Ty's having with his website now that he's adding an online store with *Undercover Ops* merch.

It's only as I'm walking home that Ty's question about my most recent ex resurfaces along with that curious niggling feeling, and then the pieces fall into place. I met Lauren right after my regular partner at the time got engaged, but I didn't go out with her until after Ty and Cam got together. There'd been a stupid bet right before Valentine's Day about whether, now that I was single, I could get a date before Ty got a date with Cam. I lost.

Which meant I'd been the recipient of a great deal of teasing and joking that my reign as the hookup king was coming to an end.

I don't think Lauren was a response to that, but you never know how things like this can affect you even if you're not aware of it. Lauren, of course, turned out to be a disaster. Full props to Cam for folding himself right into our friend group from the moment he met us. Lauren had flat out refused and then tried to keep me from seeing them. She became incredibly controlling, and—truth—her anger scared me, but I saw the warning signs and broke things off. Then, she trashed my car, and I called the police.

It's totally understandable that I've kept to hookups since then. Except, my dry spell, such as it was, started before her. There'd been a guy I'd been into the night our group met Cam for the first time, but I'd been so distracted watching Ty with Cam that he'd lost interest and left. Then there was Lauren, with whom I jumped into exclusivity without taking the time to really get to know her. Failure-to-launch guy had been my first attempt at hooking up since Lauren left my life in a blaze of glory and handcuffs.

"Maybe you're tired of meaningless hookups and relationships that don't go anywhere."

Ty's words come back to me, but I shake my head at them. I like sex. It's that simple. And I like sex no matter how I can get it. Hookups, friends with benefits, boyfriends or girlfriends, partners, whatever. I mean, I'm only twenty-five, I should have plenty of years left to fuck around before I really get serious about settling down.

But then I think about the look on Ty's face when Cam sent him a silly text as we were wrapping up our meeting, and my heart gives a twinge.

"Ooof! Sorry." I've been so distracted by what's going on in my head, I've run into a guy standing in front of my building. Despite the fact that he's very good looking, and I catch the flare of attraction in his gaze, my attention is drawn to the flyers he's holding in his hands and fuck me if the face on those flyers isn't the guy I couldn't get it up for.

Four

Aaron

I know something about your brother. Can we meet for coffee?

I stare at the text and try not to let hope flare in my chest. We've been through this at least a dozen times already because the reward for information my parents have offered has succeeded in bringing in a ton of tips. My parents have passed all of them—even the one from the psychic who said a clue to Zack's death could be found in Alamo Square under one of the cypress trees—onto the police. Unfortunately, most of them are from people just hoping for the reward money. I won't say they're out and out lying, but they sure as shit don't know anything about Zack's murder.

Reading the text again, I shake my head and call Kit.

"Tell me again about the guy who ran into you two nights ago," I say without preamble.

Kit sighs. I've asked him for these details at least four times since he told me about the encounter. "Like I told you before," Kit pauses long enough for me to make an encouraging sound so he'll keep talking. "The guy just ran into me. He wasn't texting or scrolling on his phone, wasn't doing anything but walking and not paying attention. From the way he checked me out, definitely into guys, gave me a good once-over, but when he saw the flyers in my hand, he went as pale as Snow White's ass, grabbed a flyer and took off."

"What did he look like?" I ask. I've flipped back to the text from the unknown number and stare at it as Kit describes a good-looking guy with dark hair and blue eyes, about five ten, built but not a gym rat. Of course, this won't help me figure out if this text is a legit lead, but as he talks, I can see this guy in my mind and know he's exactly Zack's type.

"Why the interest in some weird rando?" Kit asks.

"I got a text this morning, and I'm thinking it's from him. Says he knows something about Zack, not the murder, but Zack, and he wants to meet in person."

"Uh, you're not thinking about doing that, are you, Nancy Drew?"

"If he's legit, I'd be an idiot not to."

"And if he's some psycho headline chaser who gets his kicks from tormenting the families of murder victims? They're out there, you know. I hear about them all the time on my true crime podcasts."

I try not to roll my eyes. Since Zack's death, Kit has become obsessed with bingeing those shows. When I mentioned it to my sister, wondering if it was healthy, she told me everyone processes grief in their own way. This is Kit's, and I should leave him alone according to Shayna.

"If you do meet him," Kit continues, "I'm coming with you." And then he gasps. "What if he's actually the murderer?"

When I can't persuade Kit that it's highly unlikely this guy is the one who killed Zack—*"Do you know how many times the murderer inserts themselves into the investigation in some way?" he'd asked*—I agree to meet the guy in a public place and let Kit be in the vicinity to observe. And then I arrange to meet the guy who texted me for coffee.

I RECOGNIZE HIM AS soon as he walks through the door, and see Kit do the same from his vantage point at a table on the other side of the space. Even if Kit hadn't seen him the day he'd grabbed a flyer and ran, we're both well aware that Zack had a type, and this guy fits that to a T right down to the faded and strategically torn skinny jeans, the old band shirt, and a black jeans jacket. His brown leather shoes are a step up from the sneakers I expect, but he's definitely Zack's type. And mine, for that matter, when I'm actually attracted to someone.

I signal to him, and he tips his chin at me, then points at the counter to indicate he wants to order something first. Nodding, I glance at Kit and wish the book he's holding was less obviously a prop. Where did he even find a bodice ripper romance? And is that actually *Fabio* on the cover?

"Hey, sorry I was a bit late."

The guy slides into the seat across from me which puts his back to Kit, making it impossible for Kit to see the guy's reactions to my questions. We didn't really think this all the way through, but there's nothing for it now.

"No worries," I say and hold out my hand. "I'm Aaron. I'm Zack's older brother."

"Zack..." the guy says quietly, then reaches out to shake my hand. "I'm Nick, and...um...I think I might be the last person who saw your brother alive."

My eyebrows almost reach my hairline before my brain fully kicks in with the voice of reason. There is no way this guy—Nick—is telling me he killed Zack. He must realize how his words sounded to me because he looks horrified.

"No, no," he says quickly. "Before that. We...Zack and I..." He takes a breath and glances at me. "We—"

"Hooked up," I say.

Nick looks relieved that I've named it and sits back just as his coffee is delivered to the table along with a delicious-looking tart that smells as incredible as it looks. Or maybe that's Nick who smells so good, spicy with a touch of vanilla. Internally, I roll my eyes at myself. Now is not the time to be checking out one of Zack's randos. No matter how good looking he is.

"Yeah," Nick says, nodding his head. "We found each other on an app, and I actually didn't even know his name until I saw the flyer. He left my apartment...when we were done, and that's all I can tell you. I wish I knew more."

Disappointment makes my shoulders sag. I knew it was too much to hope that Nick would be the key to unraveling this entire mystery, but still I had hoped. As much as I think he's being truthful, though, I get the feeling he's holding something back.

"Any little thing could help us figure out what happened, so thank you," I say.

"It's not really anything." Nick picks up his fork, then puts it back down, picks up his coffee and takes a sip.

"It's more than we knew before," I say softly. "Now we know where he was coming from."

I study Nick's face as he glances around the coffee shop and see the moment he recognizes Kit. He looks confused, but then his brows crease, and he glares at me as he gestures at Kit. "Backup?" he asks.

Resigned, I wave Kit over. "For whatever's about to happen, I apologize," I say as Kit gathers up his things and bounds over to us. "He's been listening to true crime podcasts as a way to deal with his grief."

Kit slides into the seat next to me. "What's up?" he asks.

"You are a terrible undercover operative," I tell him.

With a shrug, Kit extends his hand toward Nick. "Hi, I'm Kit, Zack's best friend."

Nick slowly reaches out and takes hold of Kit's hand. "Nick."

"He hooked up with Zack," I say.

"I live in Hayes Valley," Nick adds. "About a block away from where...well..." He coughs. "Yeah."

"So, he was coming from your place," Kit says. "Where did you guys meet up?"

"Kit!"

"No, it's okay," Nick says. "If it was me, I'd want to know everything as well." He turns so he's facing Kit full on. "We matched on Grindr. I was in Spike's and Zack was around the corner. I had my car, so I drove us back to my place."

"Did you guys have anything to drink when you got there? Smoke anything?"

"We had wine that neither of us finished." Nick's eyes turn icy as he stares at Kit. "Do you want to know what positions we used as well?"

Kit smiles, but it's his snarky, bitchy smile, and I can tell this will all go sideways if Kit lets loose with a biting comment. Without thinking, I reach across the table and take hold of Nick's wrist. "I'm sorry. Kit is..." I glare at him, then turn my attention back to Nick. "We're all struggling to figure out what happened to Zack and deal with his death. Some of us are coping better than others."

With a snort, Kit sits back in his chair and folds his arms over his chest. "I can tell you're not telling us everything you know. So, I'm warning you, if you hurt this family, if you come after them or try to con them in anyway..."

"Enough," I say. "I think I can handle it from here, Kit, you can leave."

He stares at me for a long moment before he gathers up his things and stands. "Call me when you're done."

I wave him off but don't say anything until he leaves the coffee shop. I'm half expecting him to turn at the last minute and do that "I'm watching you" move pointing from his eyes to Nick, but he doesn't. When it's clear he's left, I turn back to Nick.

"Sorry about that."

"He's pretty intense."

"Yeah. He and Zack go back to like preschool, I think." I shake my head. "We were all a bit protective of Zack, which looks like it didn't end up mattering in the end."

"Hey." Nick reaches across the table and lays a hand on my arm. His hand is warm and a few sparks run across my skin from the contact. "You can't blame yourself. From what I saw, Zack was perfectly capable of taking care of himself." Pulling his hand back, he winces. "Sorry. Was that awkward for you? I'm not sure what's proper etiquette here."

"It's fine," I say and smile at him. When Nick smiles back, I'm struck by how gorgeous he is with vivid blue eyes framed by long, dark lashes. "I'm well aware of who my brother was and the way he lived his life."

That seems to help Nick relax a bit. "I really wish there was more I could tell you," he says.

"You guys didn't talk about anything? Zack didn't happen to tell you where he was going after he left your place?" I already know the answers to my questions, but I have to ask anyway.

Nick shakes his head. "We didn't really talk. I'm sorry."

"In a way, it would have been stranger if you had."

"Yeah," Nick agrees, but I hear a note of regret in his voice. He lifts his head and stares at the door. "I guess hookups weren't unusual for either of us."

"That was pretty much all Zack did," I say. "He never wanted anything long-term, said he was aromantic and didn't see the point in romantic relationships."

With a shake of his head, Nick gives out a bitter laugh. "Sounds like Zack and I would have gotten along well. Now, I wish..."

"Wish what?" I ask.

Another shake of his head dismisses my question. "Nothing." He glances at my face and then away.

The silence between us is awkward, but I can tell I'm not going to get anything else out of Nick at the moment. I meant what I said to him, the smallest detail could be important, so I'm not willing to walk away without letting him know he can contact me if he thinks of something I should know. I dig my wallet out from my back pocket and extract one of my business cards.

"I know it's weird, finding out about Zack, but if anything else occurs to you or you just want to talk, feel free to get in touch with me." I hand him the card. "It helps knowing where he was before he...yeah, and that you weren't an asshole." Sputtering as soon as the word is out of my mouth, I try to apologize but Nick is laughing as he takes my card. The sound is light and melodic, happy notes that warm my heart for a moment.

"It's okay," Nick says. "I understand what you mean, and I'll let you know if I think of anything." He slips the card into a pocket on the front of his messenger bag. "Though I had your number already because of the flyer."

"Oh, right. Yeah." I rub the scruff on my chin to cover my embarrassed smile. "Anyway...I should go."

"Sure." Nick holds out his hand. "It was nice to meet you, Aaron. I wish it could have been under better circumstances."

I shake his hand, our contact lingering a touch longer than necessary, and then get out of the coffee shop as quickly as I can. Even though I can't see him, I'm conscious of Nick's attention on me as a walk to the door. Despite telling myself not to, once I'm standing on the sidewalk, I look back and our gazes meet. Nick nods at me. He's not hiding that he was watching me, and I like that, like that he has the confidence to be upfront and own his actions. Whatever else I've found out today, the one thing I'm pretty sure I know is that Nick is not Zack's killer. Now I just have to convince Kit of this.

Five

Nick

"Remind me again why you're here," Roman says with faux irritation.

I roll my eyes and nudge the takeout coffee cup towards them. In truth, I don't really know why I made a beeline for the bookstore as soon as I finished my pastry at Loquat, but the conversation with Aaron left me unsettled, and Roman's always been the best person for helping me sort shit out.

Unfortunately, all I've been able to do since walking in the door is hand Roman a coffee and lean on the counter and talk about nothing. It's the middle of the day, no one is in the store, but I know Roman's got inventory to do and special orders to fill. They're something of a book detective and have a reputation throughout the city as the person you go to when you want to find rare books or need information on a specific edition or whatever else people who collect old books require.

"I brought you coffee," I say. "That's got to count for something." Roman shakes their head and motions toward the back room where I know they've got a fancy coffee machine and a million types of special coffee. I sigh. "You remember Min talking about that guy who was murdered in my neighborhood a couple of weeks ago?"

"The one whose family is passing out flyers because the police don't have any leads?"

"Yeah. So. Turns out, I'm a lead. Not that it helps much except to give them a better estimate of the time Zack—that was the guy's name, which I didn't even know—was killed."

Roman raises their eyebrows at me. "Do go on."

I rest my forearms on the counter and lean my weight on them. "Zack and I hooked up the day he was killed. It's very likely it happened right after he left my place, and it's kind of freaking me out." I grimace. "Not that I'm trying to make this about me, or anything. It's just...ever since I saw the flyer with his picture on it, my brain won't shut off. If we hadn't matched on the app. If he hadn't come back to my place. If I'd been able..." Biting back the rest of that sentence, I cover by taking a sip of my coffee, but I should have known Roman would pick up on my discomfort and nudge at it.

"If you'd been able to...what?" they ask.

I put my head down on the counter and whisper, "Get it up."

"I'm sorry, what?" Roman asks, and I roll my head to the side and glare up at them.

"You heard me."

"I know, but it...surprised me." Roman shrugs. "I'm not sure what the big deal is. I mean, couldn't you have talked instead of him leaving?"

The sincerity with which Roman says this makes me laugh. It's a genuine laugh because I know Roman truly doesn't understand why once sex was no longer a possibility, there hadn't been any reason for Zack to stick around, but talking is much more intimate than fucking.

"I suppose we could have," I say. "But that wasn't why we were at my place. And then...I just wanted him out of there so I could feel my humiliation in private. He wasn't in a hurry to stick around either. Now I'm wondering if we'd been able to...if I'd been able to do what we'd planned on doing, if he'd still be alive because he wouldn't have walked out my door at that moment and run into someone who hurt him. It's fucked up, and I can't get it out of my head."

"That's not your fault, you know."

"I do." I touch my head. "Up here, at least." Then I lay a hand over my heart. "In here's a different matter. There's this whole weirdness of knowing I'm probably the last person he talked to. Like, after I saw the flyer, I couldn't even look at my couch because that was where we...*almost* had sex, and it was strange to think he'd been right there. And then I have to wonder...It's just..." I shrug. "...and I don't know what to do with these thoughts."

Glancing around the bookstore to try and shake some of my unease, I admire what Roman's done here. It's a modern but cozy space with room in the back that can be used for readings and events, and it's the perfect place for them. Right now, though, I'd give anything to be at a bar with a drink in front of me and the distraction of a hundred conversations buzzing around us because that would mean I wouldn't be the sole focus of Roman's attention.

"Ty said something the other day," I say without looking directly at them. "That maybe my issue was because I'm tired of meaningless hookups with random people."

"Ty thinks romantic relationships are the answer to everything right now," Roman says. "I'm not saying he's wrong, at least not for him, but I think he's a bit biased at the moment."

I snort in response. "Probably."

"But the better question is if you think he might be onto something."

"Maybe." I stall for time by taking a sip of coffee. "I was happy fucking around until Ty found Cam."

Roman fixes me with their intense hazel gaze, and I can see the questions forming in their mind. Fortunately, the bell over the door tinkles as someone enters the store. When Roman glances in that direction, their face flushes and they bite their lower lip. I can't help it, I have to see who's caught Roman's attention and am surprised to see a conventionally attractive, slender guy with shaggy blond hair trying to act casual as he looks at the display of newly released fiction.

"Anything you want to share with the rest of the class, Ro?" I ask, keeping my voice quiet so only they can hear me.

"No."

"Want me to leave?"

"No."

The object of Roman's attention continues to browse, but he glances over at the counter as he moves on to new nonfiction and then history. Roman tracks his movement like I've ceased to exist. Once the guy disappears around a corner, Ro's gaze switches to the CCTV monitor, and they relax.

I'm about to say something when Roman cuts me off.

"Just don't, okay?" they say, and I mime locking my lips, which only makes Roman roll their eyes. "You know I'm ace not dead, right?"

"Of course," I say. "And just because I'm probably aro doesn't mean I'm a heartless, commitment-phobic asshole."

We laugh, and I push away from the counter. "I'll leave you to it, then."

"You don't have to go."

With a glance at the monitor, I shrug. "Eh. I've taken up enough of your time with my neurosis. Plus, I need to get some work done today."

"You know, it's perfectly normal to be weirded out by what happened," Roman says gently. "Or, to feel as if you could have changed the outcome and kept this guy from getting killed." When I give them a lopsided smile, they shrug. "Got to make some use of that psych degree."

I'm grinning as I walk out the door and turn toward home. It's a perfect winter day: clear and crisp with a bright blue sky and a snap in the air. As I walk through the Castro and the Lower Haight, my hand drifts into my coat pocket where I put Aaron's card. I didn't need it since I got his number off the flyer and stored it on my phone, but I like thinking he wanted to make sure I had it.

My phone vibrates, and I pull it out, surprised to see Aaron's name on the screen.

"Hey, it's Nick."

"Yeah. Hi. This is Aaron. Zack's brother."

I smile at the way he fumbles through the words. "Yes," I say. "I remember. I just saw you a little over an hour ago."

"Oh, yeah. Hey. Right."

I don't know why he seems nervous, but it's adorable.

"Is there something I can do for you?" I ask.

"Sort of," he says. "I know this is kind of an imposition, but, uh, the police would like to talk to you. I'm sorry I didn't think of it earlier."

"No worries," I say. "I should have contacted them myself. I'll call them in the morning."

"Actually..." Aaron sighs. "They'd like to interview you at your apartment. Today."

That gives me a moment of pause, but I don't have anything to hide. Zack was in my place for a grand total of maybe forty-five minutes. I poured us glasses of wine neither of us had any interest in. We made out. We groped each other. Zack got my pants undone and his hand around my cock, and...that was the end of it. "Sure. I'm still out, but I'll be home in half an hour. Is that okay?"

"I'll let them know. And, thanks, Nick, I appreciate how willing you are to help out."

"Whatever I can do. I mean that. If I were in your place, I'd want answers, too, so if I can help you out, I'm willing to do so."

Silence greets me from the other end of the line, and I'm about to check if the call dropped when Aaron draws in a shaky breath. "That's really great of you," he says, his voice tight. "If there's anything I can do in return, just ask."

Now it's my turn to pause, but my mouth barrels ahead before my brain can fully engage. "Could you tell me about Zack?" I ask, instantly regretting the request because it might sound morbid or like I'm some creepy crime chaser.

"As in...?"

"I don't know. I'm having kind of a hard time with the idea that I was the last person to see him, and I haven't got a clue who he was. I mean, I didn't even know his name until I saw the flyer. It's a bit of a head trip, and I can't stop wondering about him."

Aaron chuckles darkly. "I suppose that would be kind of strange." He clears his throat. "So, yeah, basic stuff. Zack was twenty-eight..."

By the time I reach my building, Aaron's filled me in on the rough outline of Zack's life, which is about as different from mine as you could imagine. Parents still together, siblings, family vacations filled with cousins and grandparents, a cabin in Tahoe, school at Berkeley, while my parents divorced when I was in first grade, I'm an only child, and my degree is from San Francisco State.

Along the way, I got bits and pieces about Aaron who is the oldest. Zack was the baby, and the middle child and only girl is Shayna, who's now married with two kids and living in Mill Valley. Most of Aaron's stories feature his siblings or cousins, and maybe that's because I asked him to tell me about Zack, but it also seems like he took his role as big brother to heart. I can hear the affection in his voice as he talks about Zack, and his grief as well. The one thing I don't hear, even when he tells me about the number of guys Zack hooked up with, is judgment.

"I wish he'd been more careful," Aaron says as I open the door to my apartment. "I mean, the police think this was a robbery gone wrong, so it doesn't look like his death had anything to do with his...social life, and even if it did, it still doesn't mean he deserved it or...whatever." Aaron gives a rueful chuckle. "Sorry. I'm rambling. It's been nearly three weeks, and we just want to know what happened to him. It's difficult to deal with the fact that we might never find out."

"I can imagine." I pause at a loss about what to say next. I mean, I'm having a hard time with Zack's death, so it's got to be worse for the people who knew him, loved him, worried about him, and lost him.

"I'm grateful you're so willing to help. You could have ignored the flyer or blown us off and told us it's not your problem."

"No, I couldn't. Once I saw that flyer, there was no way I couldn't contact you and let you know what I know. I only wish I was able to help more."

"You're helping. I don't know if this is going to sound weird, but...I'm glad my brother's last hookup was with someone like you."

Aaron's words stop me cold in my living room, and I stare at the couch. "Some random who didn't even know his name?" And, yeah, there's bitterness in my voice. I've been with plenty of people I wouldn't recognize on the street the next day let alone remember their names.

"No. Someone who cared enough about him to reach out and help find who killed him even though there's nothing in it for you. That tells me you're not a jerk, and I'm glad about that for Zack's sake."

"Don't make me out to be too much of a saint," I say. "I've been an asshole in the past. I could give you references if you'd like." When Aaron laughs, the sound sends warm tendrils through my body, and I smile stupidly at my phone. "At the risk of oversharing, I wish I could tell you Zack had a really good time with me, but we didn't get any further than making out."

"Oh. That paints a different picture than the one I had in my head."

"I figured. And totally all on me." I don't know why I'm telling him this, but it seems important. "Zack was great about it, probably would have stayed if I hadn't been so embarrassed." As soon as those words are out of my mouth, I hope Aaron doesn't recognize the implication. That if I hadn't been in such a rush to get Zack out of my apartment, he might still be alive.

"It's not your fault, Nick," he says.

"So people keep telling me. Can't help but feel like it is." An awkward silence fills the space between us. "Look. I'm home now, I'm gonna be here the rest of the day doing work. If you give me the name of the investigator, I'll give them a call and set up a time for them to come talk to me."

After Aaron gives me the name and number for the SFPD homicide detective in charge of Zack's case, we hang up. I continue to stare at the couch, but I'm not thinking about Zack. My thoughts drift to Aaron and the snippets of information I picked up about him as he told me about his brother, the way he seemed so sure I wasn't an asshole, and how his voice has calmed me, made it possible for me to breathe again for the first time since I saw that flyer. Even though I know it's a bad idea, I want to see Aaron again and learn more about *him* not his brother.

Stuffing that thought down, I call the detective. When I get her voicemail, I stumble over my words as I try to politely say, "Yeah, I was the guy who was supposed to fuck Zack before he was killed around the corner from my place." Then I slump down on my couch and stare at my blurred reflection on the blank TV screen. I'm just a smudge of light in the center, and it's only the fact that I know what I'm looking at that lets me know those colors are me. This whole situation is so fucked up.

I should get some work done, but my mind isn't on computers and code and fixing the stupid problems people cause for themselves. Without thinking, I cycle through my apps, mindlessly scrolling past the photos and profiles of people looking for sex, for dates, for the potential of something long-term. I swipe left on all of them because all I can think about is Zack and how our paths intersected because we both swiped right. No, what happened to him isn't my fault, and it isn't some cosmic judgment on either of us, but the decisions we made put us on this path and now I've got no choice but to follow wherever it's taking me.

Six

Aaron

In the two weeks since I met Nick and learned he was Zack's last hookup, the case hasn't moved forward an inch. Despite the flyers Kit and I have passed out, the money my parents have offered for information, and Nick's interview with the police, we have nothing. No one, it seems, saw a thing while my brother's life came to an end.

We can tell the case has been moved to the police's back burner as the number of officers investigating dwindles. If there isn't a break soon, it's going to be officially declared inactive and passed onto the cold cases department. I can't stop thinking about that and wishing there was something I could do to stop it from happening.

I also can't stop thinking about Nick. I want to see him again, but I can't come up with a plausible reason to do so even for myself. It's not like Nick had been a part of Zack's life or has more information that could help the investigation.

Despite Kit's skepticism, the police cleared Nick of any involvement after they located a single security camera that picked up my brother just after he left Nick's apartment within ten minutes of when Nick said they parted ways. The texts with Zack on Nick's phone confirmed the rest of Nick's story about how they met up and ended up back at his place. So there's no need for me to talk to Nick again. End of discussion.

And yet, I find myself staring at his phone number or opening up a text box at least once a day. I think about him far more frequently and tell myself I want to talk to him because he seemed so bewildered by the situation, so off-balance. But I know that's not the only reason.

When we met at the coffee shop, my first impression was that Nick was exactly the kind of guy my brother went for: good-looking, dresses well, on the athletic side, groomed but definitely masculine, self-assured, intelligent, and, most likely, sure of himself sexually. Everything I have always longed for in a boyfriend for myself, and everything I watched my brother find and then discard without a second thought. He never did repeats.

I didn't begrudge Zack his libertine lifestyle or judge him for it, and freely admit to being a bit of a voyeur when he told me about his latest hookups. At times, I'd even tried to emulate him, asking him to help me set up accounts on the apps he used to find men, but my results were disasters. A handful of unsatisfying dates and unfulfilling sex, and also a few run-ins with horrifying personal hygiene made me decide the apps weren't for me. My scorecard for going to clubs was even worse. I lacked whatever freedom or confidence or whatever it was Zack possessed that allowed him to share his body with random men whose names he didn't even know. I'm simply not cut out for casual, and unfortunately, I get the feeling Nick isn't cut out for anything else just like Zack was, so I put my head down and try to concentrate on work and dealing with my brother's death.

It's a good plan, except that I can't stop thinking about Nick. I can almost hear Zack in the back of my mind telling me it's because I need to get laid, but I don't think that's what it is. And, of course, then there's Kit's voice telling me I'm an idiot. I don't have to even imagine that one because he flat out told me to my face that I need to stop thinking about Nick the one time I said I wanted to check in on him and see how he was doing.

"I know what you're doing, Aaron," he'd said. "But it's not going to bring Zack back or make you feel closer to him."

I didn't think my desire to see Nick again had anything to do with Zack, but then Kit said I needed to let Nick move on as well. I couldn't argue with that, so I forced myself to stop pulling his number up or looking at our brief text chain. Mostly, I succeeded, but there were days when something would call him to mind, and I was right back to thinking about our conversation when he asked me to tell him about Zack and the way he sounded so confused and sad. I wanted to know that he was doing okay. And I wanted to know what he looked like when he was happy. I'll bet those incredible blue eyes sparkle and his plush lips would look glorious when he really smiled.

EVENTUALLY, THE DEMANDS OF my job force thoughts of Nick to the back of my mind as a supply line glitch in Asia has me scrambling to find a new source for a crucial part for one of our respirators. It's Friday evening before I've gotten everything worked out, assured my bosses and our clients that things are running smoothly again, and finally turn off my computer.

I collapse on the couch and stare blindly out the window without really seeing anything. It's a pretty uninspired view overlooking Leavenworth Street and showing me nothing of the city's skyline except another blocky building of apartments just like mine, so I'm not missing much, especially since it's already dark outside.

A quick glance at my phone tells me it's after eleven at night, which explains why my mind and body are exhausted. I also haven't showered in two days or really eaten anything resembling a meal in about as long, simply grabbing whatever I can from the fridge and heading back to the loft and my computer. At least I had the foresight to place an Instacart order as soon as I saw the supply issue develop. If I hadn't, I'd probably have been existing on pot noodles and coffee today. I've been through this before and know the drill, and know I should get up, get something to eat because as soon as the adrenaline wears off, I'll crash hard.

I grab the remote and turn on the TV, scrolling through the list of movies until I find something I've seen enough times it won't matter if I zone out but will occupy my attention just enough to ease me back into the real world. Like I said, this isn't my first rodeo, and I know what to expect when the hyperfocus bubble I've been living in for the past two days fades, and my dopamine-depleted brain starts doomscrolling in a desperate attempt to fuel itself. At the moment, though, my brain is too buzzed to think about food, and my body doesn't care.

An hour later, I'm still sitting in the same place on my couch when my phone buzzes with an incoming call, and I see Nick's name flash on the screen. I grab the phone and answer the call, a sudden surge of energy bringing me to my feet as I say hello.

For a moment, the only thing I hear is club music, and I wonder if this is a butt dial, but then...

"Aaron? Can you hear me?" It's Nick, shouting over the music.

"Yeah," I say, my voice echoing in my apartment. "Are you okay?"

"What?"

I press the phone tighter against my ear as if that will help Nick hear me over the noise of wherever he is. "Are. You. Okay?"

"Yeah, yeah. Yes. Hang on."

Closing my eyes, I concentrate on the sounds I'm hearing. It's definitely Nick saying something but he's not talking to me, and I can't make out anything distinct except for, "...keep him...doing anything...fucking..." There's the cacophony of people talking and the music, and then a voice that sounds like Kit yelling something indistinct.

"Where are you?" I ask, but Nick's still talking to someone.

I pull the phone away from my ear and text him. **What's going on?**

Instead of an answer, he hangs up. I call back, but the call rings over to voicemail. A sudden thought makes me dial Kit's number.

"Hey, it's Kit. Sorry I missed you. If you're calling to sweep me off my feet, leave a message. If you're calling to sell me something, fuck off."

Tossing the phone on my couch, I pace over to the window and run my hands through my hair. My heart's pounding in my chest and my hands are cold. I bring them to my mouth and blow on them hoping to warm my fingers and slow my breathing as I flash back to the frantic call I got from my mom asking if I knew where Zack was.

This is different, I tell myself. Nick called me. If that was Kit in the background, he was alive. They were at a club. *Fuck*. It's more likely that Kit took a swing at Nick than either one of them being seriously injured.

When my phone rings again, I lunge for it, hitting Reply and sweeping it up to my ear in the same movement.

"What's going on?" I ask, close to yelling into the phone at the same time Nick tells me everything is okay.

"I've got Kit, and I'm taking him to my place," Nick says.

I immediately register that the club noise is gone but then feel a stab of anger. "Did you call to tell me you're hooking up?"

"Fuck no. I'm telling you he's drunk off his ass, and I don't know where he lives, so I'm taking him home with me until he's sober enough not to do something he'll regret."

"He lives in the Sunset," I say as I hear Kit muttering in the background.

"That's like a hundred bucks on a Friday night, and I live five minutes away from the club."

"I'll get him," I say. "Tell me your address. I can be in Hayes in about fifteen minutes."

I'm already in motion as Nick rattles off his address, typing it into Google Maps before I've even picked up my keys. And then I'm out my door, running down the three flights of stairs to the garage below my building, thankful I pay the extra money for a dedicated parking spot because parking in this neighborhood is a pain in the ass.

The whole way to Nick's place, my mind is a mess wondering what Kit's gotten himself into, hoping he's okay, beating myself up that I've been so self-absorbed in my and my family's grief that I haven't noticed what Kit's going through. There's also a small part of me that's looking forward to seeing Nick again, but I don't let myself think about that as I concentrate on driving.

It isn't until I'm pulling into a parking place around the corner from Nick's building that I recognize how close I am to where Zack died. The fact that he wasn't at the top of my thoughts hits me so hard I stop moving. *Fuck*. Up until two days ago when work exploded into a blizzard of meetings and phone calls and searching out new suppliers as I tried to fix the break in our supply chain, Zack was pretty much the only thing I'd thought about for the past five weeks. I have a moment of panic as I realize I haven't checked in with the police, I haven't been handing out flyers. Besides answering a few texts, I haven't checked in with my parents or sister either.

I feel like I've let everyone down, and by the time I'm knocking on Nick's door, I just want to go home and crawl into bed.

"You don't look much better than Kit," Nick says as he steps back from the door to let me into his place.

Running a hand through my hair, I shake my head trying not to notice how hot Nick looks in his clubbing clothes. He's wearing black skinny jeans that show off his long legs, a shimmery black button-down shirt that gives the illusion of being see-through. Or, it might be see-through. I can't tell because I force myself to look away from him and take in the compact kitchen just to my right.

"Thanks for calling me," I say. "What happened?"

Nick closes the door and leads me past the kitchen and a small dining area which opens into a living space with a large window that overlooks Gough Street. Kit is sprawled on the couch, one arm thrown over his eyes, mouth open, clearly asleep or passed out. The blanket Nick has covered him with is carefully tucked around him, and there's a bottle of Gatorade on the coffee table within easy reach for when Kit wakes up.

"Is he okay?" I ask, but I don't move away from Nick. I can feel the warmth radiating off him, and it settles something in me.

"Far as I can tell." He shrugs. "Some friends dragged me out to Prowl tonight because I haven't...not since..." Another shrug as he worries at his lower lip with his front teeth. He gestures at Kit. "Anyway...he was there, drunk or high or whatever, but obviously in no condition to give consent for anything, so we got him out of there and brought him here because it was the closest place we could think of."

"Yeah. Thanks. He's been having a really rough time since Zack died."

"I get that. I don't know what I'd do if that happened to one of my friends."

The emotion in Nick's voice brings my focus back to him, and I take advantage of the fact that he's staring at Kit to really look at him. *Fuck, he's gorgeous.* I am suddenly very warm, but that's probably because I haven't taken off my coat and I pretty much ran here from my car. Taking a deep breath, I give voice to the reasons I think Kit is taking everything so hard.

"He had to cancel plans with Zack that night, so he's been blaming himself for Zack being in Hayes Valley."

"That's not his fault," Nick says. "But I know how he feels."

He purses his lips, and I know he's thinking about his own, similar feelings about the timing of Zack's death. "It's not your fault either," I say softly, and Nick gives a small nod. Then I give voice to the other reason for Kit's devastation. "I always suspected he was in love with Zack," I say, pitching my voice low even though I'm pretty sure Kit's still out of it. "Zack thought the only reason to have a relationship was so you could have sex on the regular, but since he never lacked for partners…" I trail off as Nick turns to face me, and I draw in a sharp breath at the hurt I see there. "There wasn't anything wrong with the way Zack lived his life," I say. "It's just that I think it killed Kit a bit every time Zack talked about a hookup."

Nick nods, shifts on his feet a bit. "You want some coffee? Tea? I don't think he's waking up anytime soon if you want a beer or wine."

There's an obvious evasion in his offer, but I tell him I'd love a cup of coffee because it gives us something to do besides watch Kit. I follow him back to the kitchen where Nick takes a mug from the rack next to the Keurig then pops in a pod and presses a button on the machine. He stares intently as it starts to gurgle, as if it won't do what he wants if he doesn't watch it closely.

When the mug's full, he hands it to me, and our fingers brush, the shock of contact almost enough to make me jerk my hand away. I don't. But I do pull back sharply enough that the hot coffee sloshes onto my wrist. I gasp at the surprise of it.

Nick hands me a paper towel, holding it out to me with two fingers as if he's trying to avoid any additional contact with me. I set the mug down on the counter and dry my hand, expecting Nick to make a second cup of coffee for himself.

"I'm going to take a shower," he says instead. "Get out of these sweaty clothes."

"Okay," I say and try not to imagine the way he'll look standing naked under the spray of water as he walks toward the stairs that lead to the lower level of his apartment.

Seven

Nick

I FIGHT THE URGE to run down the stairs to my bedroom even though my pulse is racing. I'm not sure what's made it imperative for me to get some space from Aaron—if it's his presence, something he said, or the whole fucked up reason both he and Kit are in my home—all I know is I need a moment without him in it.

By the time I'm in my shower, eyes closed and head tilted back as the falling water soothes me, I'm calmer, but there's a new issue. My dick is half-hard, and I feel the tightness of arousal in my groin and stomach, an ache of need that has me sighing as the water cascades over my body like a caress. I'm hyperaware of my skin and the fact that I haven't been touched in weeks, not since Zack. That thought should be enough to kill the boner I'm now sporting, but it doesn't. Nor does my awareness of Aaron, who's probably sitting at the table directly above me. And that thought makes me even harder.

Fuck.

Earlier this evening at Prowl, guys were grinding their asses against me, draping themselves all over me. My hands had been on their hips, my tongue in their mouths, our bodies moving like we were having sex rather than dancing and my dick had still been AWOL just like it's been for the past several weeks.

But that's not the case now.

Now, it's standing tall and proud, acting as if it's ready for some action, my body sparking to life as I trail my hand down my chest and across my abs. Coarse hair flattens under my fingers as I follow my treasure trail lower and lower until I'm touching my cock. I squeeze the base with my fingers, run my thumb along my length and graze it across my tip, hissing at how sensitive I am. Even under the water, I'm slick with precum. And, fuck, it feels good to give myself a couple of hard strokes, my blunt fingernails scraping across my balls every time my hand descends.

Before I give it too much thought, I'm jerking off, leaning against the shower tile, my breath coming hard and fast. I groan, and it echoes, so I bite my lower lip and hope Aaron didn't hear me. The thought that he might have makes my hips jut forward, my cock thrusting into my fist, my breathing turned harsh as every nerve ending in my body wakes up. I am so turned on, I wouldn't be able to stop myself even if I wanted to, and I come what would be embarrassingly fast if it wasn't one of the best orgasms I've ever had. Blinding in its intensity, my dick hard as a rock as I spill into my fist, my entire body tightens as a second wave hits me.

I rest my forehead against the tile, breathing hard as conscious thought returns. Was I too loud? Did my voice carry? Fuck. I can't believe I did that with Aaron right upstairs.

My cheeks burn as I finish washing myself, but I can't deny it's really hot to think Aaron might have heard me. That I might go upstairs to find him flushed, trying to hide that he's aroused. It would embarrass him, somehow I know that even though we haven't spent enough time together for me to know *him*. If Kit weren't passed out on my couch, he'd want to leave—I'm sure of that, too—would have already done so except he wants to take care of Kit. And, strangely, I find that thought—about how Aaron would put Kit's needs before his own discomfort—the one that stays with me as I get out of the shower and put on a clean pair of sweats.

When I get back upstairs, Kit's still asleep on the couch, and Aaron's sound asleep at the table with his head resting on his arms. I pause a moment to take him in.

Although Zack and I spent less than an hour in each other's company, I've looked at his social media pics enough to see the similarities between him and Aaron. But where Zack was all toned muscle and carefully styled and sculpted perfection, Aaron is softer with unkempt hair that curls around his face and clothing that does nothing to show off his broad shoulders and narrow waist.

Especially not tonight.

I smile as I walk into the kitchen as quietly as I can and grab myself a beer from the fridge. Not wanting to disturb either Kit or Aaron, I drink it leaning against the counter, letting the alcohol and the aftereffect of my orgasm wrap me in a cozy glow.

It feels nice having people in my space. I eye the huddled form on the couch. Okay, maybe not Kit. He was pretty much an asshole as Avy, Min, Sash, and I were trying to get him out of the club, but given what Aaron said, I can maybe forgive him. I know how much this situation has messed with my mind, I can only imagine what it's like for Zack's best friend and his brother.

Turning my attention to Aaron, that sense of warmth in my core grows stronger. It's nice having *him* here if only because he so clearly needed someone to watch over him for a bit. The sense I get from him—especially given our conversation the day I asked him to tell me about Zack—is that he's a caretaker, someone who makes sure everyone around him is safe before worrying about himself. If that's the case, Zack's death must have done a number on Aaron, so I'm happy to give him some space to relax. But it doesn't mean anything. As soon as Kit is able to get on his feet, they'll be out of my life.

I almost hear Ty's voice in my head, "Sure, Nick, whatever you need to tell yourself."

Fuck off, I tell that voice just as Aaron inhales deeply, snorts, then sits up. He rubs his eyes, clearly confused about where he is, and I push off the counter and walk over to the table.

"Want me to make a new one for you?" I ask as I reach for the mug of now cold coffee.

The confusion in Aaron's expression morphs into something that looks like happiness and affection before he sits up all the way and rubs his face.

"Sorry about that," he says. "It's been a rough couple of days at work. Not to mention..."

"Yeah," I say. "I can't imagine." I hold up the mug. "Do you want a fresh one?" Aaron nods and follows me into the kitchen. "I've also got beer, if you'd rather, or wine."

Aaron laughs. "Alcohol would probably knock me right out again. I'll stick with coffee."

As I set about making another cup, I ask him, "So, how are you doing with everything?" Out of the corner of my eye, I see Aaron startle and wonder if anyone has asked him how he's coping since Zack's death. I suspect not.

He shrugs and runs a hand through his hair. "Some days are better than others. This..." he waves a hand toward the living room where Kit still lies immobile on my couch, "...is probably the worst so far."

At that moment, Kit grumbles and rolls over. He's restless, pushing at the blanket and tossing his head, all the while making indistinct sounds. It seems like he might be having a nightmare, and Aaron immediately goes to him, placing a gentle hand on Kit's shoulder then tucking the blanket around him again once he settles.

When he returns to the kitchen, I hand him the freshly brewed coffee. "Maybe it's time to get Kit some help," he says.

"Maybe," I say, but it's not really any of my business. Except, when I really look at Aaron, I see how exhausted he is. "What about you?"

Aaron shrugs and looks down at the mug in his hands as if he just realized he's holding it.

Without thinking, I reach out and lift his chin so he has no choice but to look at me. "Who's taking care of you, Aaron?"

As soon as his eyes meet mine, everything around us fades into the background, and the only thing I know is the warmth of his skin under my fingertips, the slow part of his lips, the soft heat of his breath against my thumb as he exhales, and the pounding of my own heart. His eyes are a beautiful mosaic of greens and golds with flecks of copper near the fathomless depths of his pupils. They are full of pain, but as we stand together, something else flickers to life in them.

My body is still buzzing slightly from my orgasm, but as I touch Aaron for the first time, a different sensation takes me over. It's warmth and light, a settling of my thoughts as I draw in a deep breath. Calm takes me over as I glance at Aaron's lips. I know what arousal feels like, attraction, desire, lust, all the stages of when I want someone, but this is different. It's like those moments when I would go home with Ty after school, and we'd walk into a house smelling of fresh-baked cookies or homemade bread, and I'd tell myself this is what home feels like, and wish I could move in with him and his family because my own was such a shitshow with the endless succession of my mom's boyfriends. It's more than that, though, and I wish I was able to name it, but I've never felt anything like this before.

Aaron shifts, leaning into my hand. "No one," he says as he closes his eyes, and it takes a beat of my heart to realize he's answering my question about who takes care of him.

I want to kiss him, I realize. We're near enough, it wouldn't take much for me to touch my lips to his, but I don't. With the gentlest of strokes to his jaw, I increase the distance between us and drop my hand, not understanding why my heart aches ever so slightly at the loss of contact.

"That's not okay," I say. "You need someone, too."

There isn't time for Aaron to reply because Kit lets out a groan and begins to retch.

"Fuck," I say as I grab for the bowl I'd left on the counter for just this instance and run to the couch, Aaron a step behind me. He rolls Kit onto his side, rubbing his back and shoulders, while I position the bowl on the floor.

Between the two of us, we manage to keep Kit from aspirating on his own vomit without anything landing on my floor. I'd like to say this is the first time I've had to do something like this, but a couple of my friends have no common sense when it comes to alcohol. I'll admit that I've been in Kit's position more than a few times as well. I don't envy him the hangover he's going to have when he wakes up.

Once Kit's stomach is empty, I take the bowl away and wash it out in the sink, then come back with a wad of damp paper towels in the now clean bowl. Aaron has shifted positions so he's behind Kit, arms wrapped around him. Kit's still out of it.

"What do you think he took?" I ask as I hand Aaron the towels.

Aaron shakes his head as he takes them. "I have no idea. I'm hoping it was just molly and not something harder." He wipes the sweat from Kit's face, then cleans his mouth. I hold out the bowl so he can toss the towels in it, then pick up the bottle of Gatorade, twist off the top, and hand it to him so he can try to get Kit to drink something. "He and Zack never got into the harder stuff, but I don't know. This is so far beyond..."

Even though Aaron closes his eyes, I see the tears. I'm moving before I know what I'm doing, squeezing myself behind him with my ass on the armrest, my legs straddling him. I pull him against my chest. At first, he resists, but then he surrenders, turning his upper body to press his face into my belly. When I wrap my arms around him, he lets out a shuddering breath, and it's all I can do not to shiver in response.

This is not like me. I'm not the guy my friends turn to when they need comfort. They don't pour their hearts out to me or talk to me about issues with their boyfriends and girlfriends. And I don't either. Emotions are messy, and I don't like feeling responsible for anyone else's. It's why I prefer hookups. All my relationships have started with a casual encounter that became interesting enough to do multiple times. But that's all they were, and that's why they all ended with partners telling me I didn't care enough or pay enough attention to them. "You check out as soon as feelings get involved," one of my exes told me.

All of it is true and is why I am completely unprepared by how right it feels to have Aaron in my arms, to be giving him comfort, and how much I hate it when he pulls away.

Eight

Aaron

Oh. My. God. I cannot believe how good it feels to have Nick's arms around me. I want to live here forever as the fatigue and mind fog I've been feeling all day disappear. I would chalk it up to the catnap I had while Nick was showering, but really, I started feeling better as soon as I stepped into Nick's apartment. Something about being with him brought me back to life. And then there's the care and concern he's shown for Kit's well-being.

Mine, too, if I'm being honest with myself. When he asked who takes care of me, I just about broke down because I knew he recognized how much work I've been doing to hold everyone else together. He's not at all what I expected when we met.

Too soon, though, I get self-conscious about leaning against him. As much as I don't want to move, I feel like I should, so I fake a huge yawn and pull away from him. It's got to be my imagination that makes it seem as if he holds on until he has to let go, and I miss the feel of him immediately.

He slides off the couch, remaining close enough I feel the heat of his body.

"You've got to be exhausted," he says.

I open my mouth to deny it when another yawn—this one real—takes hold and makes it impossible to deny the truth of what Nick said. "Pretty much," I say. I look down at Kit. "He seems to be doing better. We can probably get him down to my car so you can have your place back."

Nick looks out the window as if considering what I offered.

"What if you stay here?" he asks. "I'll watch Kit, and you can get some sleep."

"It's almost three in the morning," I say. "You've got to be wiped out as well."

He turns back toward me. "I'm kind of a night owl anyway, plus I had a couple of Red Bulls and vodka after my friends dragged me out to the club, so I'm fine. I wasn't planning on getting much sleep tonight anyway." The lopsided, almost embarrassed smile he gives me just about kills me.

"I'm sorry Kit ruined your evening."

He shrugs and shakes his head. "It's fine. I was there more to be with my friends then to find a hookup." Another shrug. "I mean if the opportunity presented itself, sure, but I haven't really been looking since..."

As his voice trails off, his gaze finds mine, and I'm reminded again that Zack's death didn't just affect the people who knew him. Nick's dealing with fallout from that night as well. Maybe it's because I know he feels like he has something to make up for, that he feels as if his aborted hookup with my brother played a role in Zack's murder, or maybe it's only that I want to spend more time with him, but I agree to stay.

It takes a bit more convincing for me to accept the offer of Nick's bed, but I eventually give in on that as well and follow him down the stairs.

"That's the bathroom," Nick says with a nod to one of the three doors. "And that's my office." He pushes the third door open, and I follow him into a room that looks a heck of a lot nicer than my bedroom with soft gray walls and a king-sized Mission style bed with the fluffiest looking dark gray comforter pulled neatly across its top. The color in the room comes from the half dozen purple pillows of various sizes, shapes, and gradations that are piled against the headboard. It looks so inviting, I almost yawn again from looking at it.

"My friend Min," Nick says as he removes the decorative pillows to reveal the more functional set. "She's an interior decorator, and she always gives me pillows because I told her once they're like fat litter for your bedroom."

He sounds so put-upon that I laugh and help him remove the last two.

"The sheets are clean, but if you'd prefer, I'll get you a blanket and you can sleep on top of the comforter."

"Thanks," I say and take a moment after Nick disappears into the en-suite to really take in his room. I'm immediately drawn to a framed image hung over his dresser. It looks like...yes! It's a sketch of one of my favorite characters from *Undercover Ops*, my favorite web comic. "This is very cool," I say as he comes back into the room with a plush blanket in his arms. "I love Cypher X. I wish he was in more episodes."

"I'll let Ty know," he says. He tosses the blanket onto the bed.

"You'll let...you know the guy who does *Undercover Ops*?" I step to the side of the bed and help him spread the blanket out.

"Yeah. Ty's been one of my best friends since second grade."

"So...does that mean Cypher X is *you*?"

Nick laughs. "Kind of. I mean, I help Ty out with computer shit." He shrugs. "I do IT for law firms, but, yeah, Ty created that character after his laptop crashed, and I was able to recover everything for him." Smoothing the last wrinkle out, he nods at the bed. "Well..."

There's a moment of awkwardness as our gazes meet, and I swear Nick blushes before he says something about getting back upstairs. I nod before I do something stupid like asking him to stay.

I climb into Nick's bed as he closes the door behind himself and settle against pillows that smell like him. My mind races, suddenly wide awake, and every inch of my skin is aware that I am in Nick's bed. Feeling self-conscious, I pull one of his pillows close and wrap my hands around it, denying to myself how deeply I want to inhale the citrusy tang of Nick's shampoo, the traces of vanilla and clove from his aftershave, and the spicy, masculine scent of his skin.

Eventually, my mind slows, my body relaxes, and my eyes close. I sleep better than I have in weeks and wake to the sound of Kit chattering away upstairs.

"Hey, sleepyhead," Kit says as I emerge onto the top floor. He's standing in Nick's kitchen in what I can only assume are borrowed sweats since he wasn't wearing them last night and he sure as fuck didn't pack an overnight bag. His hair is still damp, so I assume he also took a shower. And, he's holding a spatula which I can only assume is to flip the pancakes that are cooking in a pan on the stove.

"How are you feeling?" I ask as he turns to Nick's Keurig and swaps out the used pod for a new one, then places a mug underneath and presses the button to start the coffee brewing.

"Bit of a headache, bit dehydrated, but not too bad." He lifts a bottle of Gatorade and shakes it at me. "Nick's making sure I'm drinking enough."

Nick sits on a stool at the breakfast bar, a half-finished plate of pancakes sitting in front of him. He grins at me. "Some people have all the luck," he says. "I'd probably be in bed with the covers over my head."

I laugh, and Kit places the freshly made mug of coffee in front of the stool next to Nick's. Taking that as an indication of where I'm supposed to sit, I slide onto the stool. "You're letting him cook?" I ask.

"Hey!" Kit shakes the spatula at me. "This is my way of saying thank you for taking care of me last night."

"Yeah. But who nearly burned my mom's kitchen down when he was thirteen?" Beside me, Nick snorts.

"That was Zack's fault, not mine." The playfulness disappears from Kit's voice, and he turns back to the stove, but I see the slight slump in his shoulders that doesn't come from him flipping pancakes.

Fuck.

I get up from my seat and walk over to him, put my arm around his shoulder.

"Don't," Kit says before I open my mouth. "I know what I did was stupid, okay? And that I was lucky someone was there to help." He turns his head and nods at Nick. "And I know I probably need to talk to someone before I do something that can't be undone." Bumping his hip against mine, he leans his head against my shoulder. "Thank you for taking care of me."

"It was mostly Nick."

"Don't sell yourself short," Nick says. "As soon as I called, you came right over."

"Well, thank you both," Kit says as he reaches for a plate and deposits four perfectly fluffy, perfectly round pancakes onto it, then shoves it into my hands. "Eat."

I return to the stool next to Nick, pour maple syrup over the stack, and dig in. "These are amazing," I say around a mouthful of buttery goodness. "Thank you, Kit."

Kit nods and turns back to the stove to make more pancakes because, at the rate I'm going, I will be done with these in under a minute.

"So, I was thinking," Nick says, and I pause between bites to lift my head and take him in. He looks tired, but not all that bad for having been up all night.

"Yeah?" I chase the last bite of pancake around my plate to soak up all the remaining syrup.

Nick takes a sip of his coffee and nods. "Yeah. My friends and I get together a couple of times a month for drinks and shit. Would you want to...I don't know...come out with us next time? Ty'll be there, and I can introduce you."

I damn near choke on the food in my mouth. "Seriously?" I finally manage.

Grinning, Nick nods. "Don't get any ideas though, Ty's all but engaged to this guy he met on jury duty this year. We'd be taking bets on when they'll make it official, but they started going out on Valentine's Day, so there's no point because those guys are all heart-eyes for each other. We're expecting they'll do something sappy and uber-romantic."

"That's so sweet," Kit says as he places more pancakes in front of us.

"How big a batch did you make?" I ask. "Not that I'm complaining." I fork another three onto my plate, and Nick takes the remaining one. "Sorry. Do you want...?" I indicate my stack, but Nick shakes his head.

"It's kind of sickening," Nick says. "They're all cuddled up together whenever we go out now. I mean, Cam's a great guy and all, and he fit into our group better than anyone ever has, but it's still kind of...I don't know. Ignore me. It's nice to see Ty so happy." He looks at me. "So, do you wanna?"

"Say yes, Aaron. You know you want to."

I glare at Kit, but then sigh. "You're sure it'll be okay?"

"Positive." Nick nods at Kit. "You can come, too, if you promise to stay out of trouble."

Kit finally gives Nick a look that is the pure sass I'm more familiar with from Zack's BFF. "I can't promise anything, honey, but I'll be on my best behavior."

"And that is all we can ask," I say.

"So," Kit says as soon as I start the car. "Tell me everything that happened while I was passed out."

"You don't remember anything?" I ask, and when Kit shakes his head, I glare at him. "What the fuck did you take?"

Kit shrugs. "Obviously something I shouldn't have. I'll do better reading the labels next time, dad. It fucking happens sometimes, okay?" He glares back at me. "Stop avoiding my question. What happened?"

"Nothing."

The look Kit gives me is one I'm so familiar with from Zack that my throat closes up with sudden grief. It's the look that says, "don't bullshit me," and Zack used it mercilessly when he thought I was holding something back from him.

"Nothing happened," I repeat. "We talked a bit. Nick took a shower. *Alone.* I fell asleep at his table, and he offered me his bed. *And* he stayed upstairs to watch you because there was an incident when you started puking and we had to make sure you didn't aspirate on your own vomit. He wanted to make sure it didn't happen again."

"So, you're saying, if I hadn't been there you guys would have hooked up."

"I am not saying that. If you hadn't been there, I wouldn't have been either. End of story."

"Girl, he invited you on a date."

"It's not a date. He's getting together with his friends and asked me if I wanted to join them so I could meet..." I stop speaking because Kit is grinning at me. "You know what, never mind."

We're on Fell heading toward Golden Gate Park, which is the quickest route to Kit's house. But we're now stuck in the endless progression of lights that are timed, and I'm hitting each one red because Kit distracted me too much to remember to slow down to the right speed. Silence fills the car every time I stop because I refuse to look at Kit or engage with him on this topic while he's sitting in the passenger seat smiling like I just handed him the best Christmas present ever.

"He invited you, too," I finally say which makes Kit laugh.

"How are you so bad at this?" he asks. "Inviting you out with his friends is a low-key way to spend more time with you without putting pressure on either one of you. Like, if it doesn't go well, it's no biggie because it was just hanging out. But, if it does go well, he can ask you back to his place afterward. Plus, it lets his friends check you out and sign off on you."

"It's not like that," I say. "His friend does this webcomic I like, and he offered to introduce me."

"Hm hmm. Whatever you say. I'm going to go to this friend meetup thing just to watch your face when you realize how wrong you are. That guy? He wants you."

When I scoff at the idea—because, seriously? I'm boring, and Nick is...amazing—Kit rolls his eyes. "What? You don't think you're attractive?"

"I'm okay," I say.

"Okay?" Kit's tone is incredulous. "Trust me, Aaron, you're more than okay."

Something in his voice makes me glance at him, but Kit's staring out the window as we cut through the park so I can't see his expression.

We don't talk for the few minutes left in the drive to Kit's place. I pull into a short driveway in front of the 1940s bungalow he shares with several people including three who are one half of a polycule. Kit has tried to explain the dynamics of that relationship but seeing as how I've never successfully navigated a monogamous relationship, there's no way I'd be able to handle being involved with five people at the same time.

Kit thanks me for taking care of him the night before but pauses before opening the car door. "When Nick contacts you about this friend thing, promise me you'll go," he says. "Because, in case you haven't noticed, you kind of like him back."

He gets out of the car before I can formulate an answer, closes the door, and waves to me before walking away. Watching him until he disappears inside the house, my mind is a tangle of confusion, denial, and the frustration of knowing that even if Nick wants me as Kit said, it might not mean he's looking for more than sex. And I need to know there's a possibility of more before we have a chance of anything happening between us.

Nine

Nick

My place is weirdly quiet and empty after Kit and Aaron leave. I putter around straightening up the couch and washing dishes, distracting myself from the feeling that something is missing. It isn't until I'm confronted with my empty bed that I realize it's because I've erased all trace that Aaron was in my apartment, and that feels wrong in a way I don't understand.

The blanket is neatly folded on the end of the bed, and I wish Aaron had left it exactly as it was when he woke up. I wish I could see the imprint of where his body had rested so I could see if it matched the image I'd had in my mind as I sat at my table a few hours ago and tried to get some work done while distracted by the thought of him sleeping below me.

Overwhelmed by the tiredness I'd been keeping at bay since Avy, Min, and Sash arrived at my door the previous night and basically kidnapped me, I crawl into bed and pull the blanket over myself. It smells faintly of Aaron. Or, at least what I imagine Aaron smells like because I haven't been close enough to him to be able to identify which of the scents I detected were actually his. That lack of knowledge suddenly seems like a tragic loss, and I gather the blanket around me, wrapping my hands in its thick pile and drawing my knees up into the position I'd imagined Aaron had been in.

I sleep and wake mid-afternoon to a message from Ty that we're doing brunch at Boogaloo's on Valencia at one the next day. Grinning, I text Ty privately and tell him that I might have a plus one who'll be joining us. Ty texts back a heart emoji.

It's not like that, I type back, but I pause before sending it because that isn't exactly true, is it? It *isn't* like that, but I think I'd like it to be. So, I settle for: **he might bring a friend who's a PITA** because that is true. Kit is not for the faint of heart, and I secretly hope that if Aaron joins us the next day, Kit will have something else already planned.

Got it, Ty responds, and I send a thumbs up. Then I invite Aaron to brunch and tell him where and when to find us the next day if he wants to meet Ty. And then I get my day going. There's work to do, and I need to distract myself from looking at my phone to see if Aaron had replied.

As usual when my friends get together, there's lots of hugging and excited greetings as if we don't see each other on the regular. Cam's best friend, Marney, is there with Iris, her girlfriend, so we're a big group to accommodate and still sorting out seats when Aaron arrives. With Kit. I leave everyone else to figure out seating and go greet them.

It's a little awkward because my first instinct is to hug Aaron, but I don't know how he reacts to physical contact, so I end up with my arms held out and settle for placing my hands on his upper arms. I have just enough time for the solidness of his biceps to register before Kit snorts and rolls his eyes.

"Come on over," I say and turn to the corner where our group is taking off their coats and settling into their seats. Several sets of eyes stare at me curiously, and Min is actively looking between me and Kit and then Aaron. She's got to recognize Kit from the other night. I know she's trying to do the math, and it's not adding up in a way that makes sense to her, which kind of cracks me up.

"Everyone," I say as soon as we get close enough I'm not broadcasting to the entire restaurant. "This is Aaron."

"And I'm Kit," he says before I have a chance to introduce him. "Some of you met me the other night. I just want to say that was not my finest hour but thank you for looking out for me. Nick here's an absolute prince." He leans in and kisses me on the cheek, then gives me a sly wink, and I fight not to laugh because that will give my friends something else to think about.

We have to reshuffle the seating a bit so that Aaron and I can sit next to each other. Kit winds up across from us between Dan and Sash. Fortunately, Ty is next to me, so I introduce him to Aaron, who turns an adorable shade of pink as he stammers out how much he loves *Undercover Ops*. Cam practically preens with pride as Ty thanks him, and I pick up my menu to hide the smirk on my face.

Before any of us have a chance to look at the menu and start discussing what we're going to order, a server arrives with two pitchers of mimosas and begins filling our champagne glasses.

"We didn't order this," Dan says.

"Hush, honey," Kit tells him. "When a mimosa appears in front of you, you don't ask why it's there, you drink it."

He lifts his glass, but Ty and Cam both stand up, which immediately gets everyone's attention. Even Kit, who lowers his glass back to the table.

"You're right," Ty tells Dan. "You didn't order it. We did." He snuggles into Cam's side. "Because we've got an announcement." He looks up at Cam, and the adoration in his expression makes my throat close up. Then he glances at the rest of us. "We're engaged," he says.

There's a moment of stunned silence, and then we all leap to our feet and swarm them with hugs and congratulations. We're all laughing and crying, and I'm breathless by the time I sit back down next to Aaron.

"That was unexpected," I say.

"Yeah," Min shouts across the table. "We were all thinking Valentine's Day. Like, we couldn't even do a pool because everyone picked that day. What happened?"

"You weren't wrong," Cam says. "Turns out we were thinking the same thing." He smiles at Ty.

"But..." Dan waves at them.

"We chose the same jeweler and ran into each other at the store," Ty says with a shrug. "Cam got down on one knee and proposed on the spot." He hugs Cam even tighter. "And then we chose our rings. Together."

"Of course, you did," Dan says, and we all laugh.

"I told you all it was going to be one of those really cute proposals," I say, but then look at the happy couple and tell them congratulations again, which starts another wave of congratulations and the clinking of champagne glasses.

I don't know who starts it, but we end up tapping our forks against our glasses, and cheer when Ty and Cam kiss. Everyone in the restaurant cheers or claps along with us even though we're probably being obnoxiously loud and distracting.

Eventually, we settle down, open up our menus, and discussion turns to what everyone's going to order. I notice that Aaron's gotten quiet, and at first, I think it's just the overwhelm of our group. We can be a lot to take in, especially when something exciting has happened. Ty's the first of us to take that next step into a committed relationship, and even before this latest development, Cam's inclusion in our group changed the dynamic. It also increased our numbers because we've folded Marney and Iris in as well. Even without Aaron and Kit, we take up a lot of space, so I can understand that Aaron might feel a bit lost.

After we place our orders, Sash looks around the table and asks who we think is going to be next now that we've shoved the first penguins off the relationship ice floe to test the waters. Everyone laughs, but there are quite a few glances around the table.

"Well, we sure as shit know it's not going to be Nick," Avy says, which makes everyone laugh even harder.

Beside me, Aaron shifts uncomfortably in his seat. I ignore the continuing comments about my lack of enthusiasm for committed relationships and nudge Aaron with my shoulder.

"You okay?"

"Yeah." His voice is quiet, almost a whisper, but I don't have any problem hearing him.

"You sure?"

"I'm fine." He gives me a small smile, but it doesn't hide the sadness in his eyes. At least not from me.

"Do you want to get out of here?"

He shakes his head, but he's not telling me the truth. Whatever's going on for him, I want to make it better for him if I can.

I stare at him a moment longer before making up my mind. I put my napkin on the table and stand up. "Hey, guys, Aaron's not feeling too great at the moment, so I'm going to give him a ride home."

There's a chorus of disappointment and wishes for him to feel better. I say goodbye to Ty and Cam and congratulate them again. As I turn toward the door, I catch the smirk on Kit's face and the wink he gives Aaron as he follows me away from the table.

Once we're outside and away from the restaurant's windows, I tell Aaron that I actually didn't drive. "I just wanted to get you out of there."

"Yeah. It was just...I got caught up in thinking about Zack." Aaron gives me a rueful smile. "I wish it hadn't blown my chances for really meeting Ty."

"Eh. I'm sure I can arrange another one. Maybe at a time when it's not such a huge group."

"That would be good. It was cool to be there for his announcement, though."

"They are the world's most annoying couple," I say. Without saying anything to each other, we begin walking down Valencia. "If they weren't so perfect for each other...I don't know, I might have to reconsider my friends."

Aaron laughs, and I can't help but grin at the sound.

We're moving in the direction of Hayes Valley, so I say, "My place is about a half hour walk from here. If you want, we can grab something to take back there. Or we can find somewhere else to eat if you're hungry."

"I don't know. What would you—"

"Nope. This is about you. What do you need right now?"

Aaron closes his eyes and draws in a deep breath, and I watch as his shoulders slowly loosen. When he opens his eyes again, he smiles. "I would like to go back to your place," he says. "And order something in."

"Sounds good," I say and get a genuine smile in return.

I'd be lying if I said I wasn't nervous even though I'm not sure if Aaron has anything in mind besides food. The prospect of having naked time with Aaron both thrills and terrifies me. While I am attracted to him, I'm worried that my dick will bail on me again. I've been able to jerk off a couple of times, but my stomach is a bit tied up in knots over the idea that my dick might bail on me again if Aaron and I...

I might not have to worry about it, though, because Aaron's not flirting. He's not "accidentally" bumping into me or letting his hand graze against mine as we walk, nor do I see the spark of anticipation and a sly grin when we catch each other's eye. It's just the two of us walking and talking about nothing in particular. It could be that all Aaron wanted was to get away from my friends, that being with a group that loud and excited made him miss his brother even more than he usually does.

The thought unexpectedly disappoints me.

"Do you think they're talking about us?" Aaron asks without preamble. "Back at the restaurant?"

"Would it bother you if they were?"

Aaron shakes his head. "We did leave Kit alone with them, so who knows what he'll say." His cheeks turn adorably pink and that makes me wonder what Kit's said to him. "What about you?" he asks before I can question him. "Will it bother you?"

I think about that for a moment. "Not really. I mean, me leaving with a guy isn't unusual."

"I kind of got that, but right after your friends announce they're engaged? That's cold." The smile he gives me tells me he's teasing.

"Okay. Maybe that was a little different, but..." I shrug. "It's how my friends see me. It's what they expect from me."

"But that's not really who you are, is it?"

The tone of Aaron's voice tells me he's not asking me to confirm it, he's asking the exact opposite. For some reason, I don't want to give him some bullshit answer, so I tell him truthfully that I don't know. "I guess it was who I was when we were in school, and that's what they remember." I snort. "I mean, it's not like we've been out of school for decades, or as if they've got a lot of evidence to the contrary, but..." I glance away from Aaron and look at the people around us, my eyes drawn to the couples. "I'm not sure that's what I want anymore." That statement doesn't feel strong enough, so I amend it. "I don't think it's who I want to be anymore."

Aaron nods, and we continue walking in silence for another block.

"For the record, I wouldn't be upset if they thought we left to be together," he says.

My heart beats a little faster at his words. "No?" It's the only word I can get out of my mouth.

"No." Aaron gives a quiet, almost embarrassed laugh. "Kit's gonna assume that's what's happening no matter what I tell him, but it doesn't have to be...what they think. It only has to be what we want." He clears his throat. "If the only thing happening is you helping me with a bad moment of grief, that's fine."

We're on the edge of Hayes Valley, about to cross Oak and waiting for the light to change. "Is that what you want?" I ask.

"I don't know."

"I don't know either," I say and realize I mean it. I'm in uncharted waters here, navigating a kind of attraction I've never felt before.

In the past, my interactions have been driven by a desire to fuck someone. That's all hookups are whether they're through an app or meeting someone in a club. An instant spark of sexual desire that only needs a nod or a certain look to say we're both on the same page, let's go. And once that desire is satisfied, there's no point in sticking around.

Even my longer relationships, with the exception of my first girlfriend in high school, started out like that, continuing until the sex was no longer fun or our personalities clashed too much to make it worthwhile. It's not like I didn't enjoy spending time with them, but ultimately, the only difference between my partners and my friends was the sex.

It's different with Aaron, and I've never experienced anything like it. Do I want him? Yes. Of course. He's gorgeous with dark hair and the kind of eyes I could lose myself in, and I've been dying to know what his body looks like without clothes since we met at the coffee shop. If he gave me that nod or look, I wouldn't hesitate. But I've also enjoyed talking to him, getting to know him, spending time together. I feel connected to him in a way that transcends even what I feel for my friends. I can't explain it, but I'm drawn to him as much because of that as I am by how much I'm attracted to him. The appeal of having him in my apartment isn't because we've got privacy and a bed, but because I won't have to share him with anyone else. All his words will be for me alone, and it's a bit mind-blowing that I want that as much as I want to feel his hands on me.

Ten
Aaron

I'm so aware of Nick beside me I can barely think. The warmth of his body. The scent of his cologne. The brush of his arm against mine, and the shock that runs through me when he puts his hand on my lower back as we cross Fell. It's protective. It's comforting. It's sexy as all get-out, and I love that his hand lingers when we reach the other side of the street as if he's reluctant to let me go. I nearly swoon with how perfect it feels to be with him, heading toward his apartment, and the prospect of an afternoon together. I'm a bit nervous about what he might expect, but I'm not going to let that keep me from finding out because somehow I know Nick won't push for anything that makes me uncomfortable.

This is completely opposite of how I usually am with guys. I can't even fully explain it because my experience with attraction is so limited and my track record speaks for itself. A handful of crushes that helped me figure out I was gay, maybe half a dozen hookups that taught me I wasn't into casual and needed to feel a connection with someone before my body showed any signs of interest. And connections take more time to develop than guys I've met through the apps or at bars have wanted to give me.

Maybe that's why it feels different with Nick. I'm not going to assume I know the totality of how Zack's death affected him, but it definitely has, and he's been there for me in ways not even my own family has been able to because they're mired in their own grief. I connected with Nick because of his consideration and concern, the way he took care of me and Kit and got involved when he could have walked away. The image his friends have of him as this player? That's not who I've met at all, and it's not the person who asked if I needed to leave brunch when I felt overwhelmed.

I am conflicted over how attracted I am to Nick because of Zack, though. I mean, it's not like they were boyfriends. They barely knew each other, and I remind myself Nick didn't even know Zack's name until he saw the flyer. When I think about how I would tell my family about him if things progressed for us, I get a funny feeling in my stomach. *Yeah, that guy Zack was with the day he died, yeah, I'm seeing him now.* I can't even imagine their reactions.

This is about as far from a meet-cute as I could possibly get, and I'm on the verge of telling Nick I just remembered something urgent I've got to take care of when his hand brushes against mine. Those same tendrils of excitement I felt as we crossed the street spark and fizz up my arm and make my heart beat a little quicker.

I steal a glance at him and blush when I catch him doing the same. We hold each other's gaze for a moment, then Nick glances downward, and I'm sure he's staring at my lips. I watch the tip of his tongue dart along the inside of his before he's looking into my eyes again. It's the swooniest moment I've ever had in my life, and I bite my lower lip as I duck my head because it's too much for me.

The tension between us fades as we reach Nick's building and through all the mechanics of unlocking doors, climbing stairs, entering his apartment. He takes off his coat and hangs it in a closet to the left of the front door, then holds out his hand for mine. Our fingers brush as I give it to him, and there's that shock again at this most tenuous of contact.

Nick clears his throat. "What...uh...what do you want to order?" He walks into the kitchen and opens a drawer full of take-out menus, and the contradiction of an IT guy who still collects paper menus makes me smile as I follow him.

"I don't care," I say. "I'm pretty easy."

"Are you?" Nick asks, the tease in his voice clear.

My face heats. "Sometimes."

Our gazes lock. I'm not sure either one of us is breathing. I don't know who moves first, but Nick definitely makes contact before I do, reaching out to cradle my face, his fingers brushing along my jaw, his thumb tracing the edge of my lower lip.

"Is this okay?" he asks.

"Yeah," I say and slide an arm around his waist, tentative, my hold light. "And this?"

He nods. "May I kiss you?"

"Please."

I'm sure by Nick's standards, it's pretty chaste. There's no crashing of mouths, no gasps, no frantic fumbles to pull clothing free and touch skin. Instead, it's a gentle meeting of our lips with soft caresses from Nick's fingers on the underside of my jaw. But it's mind-blowing for me. I've never felt so cherished in someone's embrace before, never felt as if a kiss was the focus, the reason someone was touching me. No further destination. No pushing for more. Simply this moment, and the two of us standing in Nick's kitchen, and knowing I don't have to worry I'm not going to be enough for him.

Nick doesn't move away when the kiss ends, he simply rests his forehead against mine and sighs. Then he laughs.

"What?" I whisper.

"None of my friends will believe we're not in bed already," he says.

I pull back slightly so I can see his expression. "Does that matter?" I ask.

"No." His thumb grazes my lower lip again, stroking slowly. He opens his mouth as if he's about to say something, then closes it and shakes his head.

"What?" I ask.

"Nothing." Stepping away from me, he points to the menus. "What do you want?"

I reach out and pull him close again. "Nick..." I say softly. "We don't have to be anything but what *we* want to be, and we don't have to figure that out right now." Feeling brave, I lift his chin with my hand and touch my lips to his. "I'm happy to be here with you and to take the time we need to figure it out together."

It's Nick's turn to pull back from me enough to see my face. His eyes move as if he's looking for something, trying to read my expression. There's fear in his. Not a lot, but it's there, and I wonder if he expected me to be disappointed in him.

"Are you okay?" I ask.

"You're not going to let me get away with anything, are you?" he whispers.

"I'm hoping you won't feel as if you have to."

He swallows hard and then melts against me, his arms going around my waist, his head nestling against my shoulder. My arms engulf him, and we rock gently against each other. When we finally part, Nick wipes his eyes and gives me a rueful grin.

"This is not what I expected when we left Boogaloo's," he says. "But I'm not sorry this is what's happened."

I smile at him. "I'm not either." Then I reach for the menus.

An hour later, Nick's coffee table is littered with the detritus of our meal. We'd agreed on Thai, and the containers in front of us hold the remnants of the garlic noodles, chili wings, and a really delicious tea leaf salad we demolished. Though we started off with some space between us, we've gravitated to the center of the couch and are now sitting thigh to thigh as we battle over the remaining noodles. Nick keeps getting his chopsticks in the way of mine, and we're both laughing. Finally, I emerge triumphant and slurp the last few noodles into my mouth, immediately aware that Nick's gaze is fixed firmly on my lips which now glisten with sauce and oil. I make a show of licking my lips, enjoying how Nick's blue eyes turn stormy, how his breath deepens, how he leans into me, then hesitates.

"It's okay," I whisper, putting my chopsticks in the now-empty container.

"Garlic breath," he says and starts to pull back from me.

Without thinking, I reach out, my hand skating along his neck, fingers creating a gentle pull to bring him closer again.

And then, we are kissing again. It's not frantic, it's not explosive. It's soft and gentle and everything I've ever wanted in a kiss. We end up lying face to face on the couch, Nick's back pressed against the cushions, his arms around me. It's a tight fit and basically means our bodies are touching from head to toes, but neither of us are acting as if we want anything more.

Even when I feel Nick's cock thicken against mine, he doesn't rock against me or change how he's kissing me. I love it. Am I aroused? Absolutely. It's how I've always dreamed things should be when I'm getting to know someone and never gotten before.

We kiss for a long time before I feel one of Nick's hands teasing at the waistband of my pants. He's not trying to go lower or undo them or anything like that, but he clearly wants something, so I pull back from him slightly, loving the way his lips are puffy and so, so red.

"What do you want?" I ask and bring one of my hands up so I can stroke his face.

Nick sighs and his eyes flutter shut. He shakes his head.

"What do you want?" I ask again, utterly enthralled by the beauty that is this man I hold in my arms. He's completely different from who I assumed him to be when we met, and I learned how similar he and Zack were. "Nick?"

"Skin," he whispers. "I want to touch you."

"Okay," I say because I know he doesn't mean he wants to get naked and move on to more athletic events. When he pulls my shirt from my waistband and strokes my back, I smile at being able to read him right. "And you?" I ask, wanting to feel him beneath my hands as well.

When Nick sighs at the touch of my palm on the smooth skin of his back, I close the distance between us so we can kiss again.

Eventually, we put on a movie and Nick grabs us a couple of beers, but we largely ignore both as our attention keeps drifting back to slow, lazy kisses and gentle caresses. I've got my head in Nick's lap, and he's running his fingers through my hair, and I realize I'm more relaxed than I've been since Zack didn't show up at our family brunch.

Without meaning to, I drift off, and when I wake up, the sun's gone down. The apartment is shadowed, the only light coming from the TV, but Nick is still stroking my head. I roll onto my back and look up at him.

"Sorry for conking out like that," I say.

"Not a problem. I kind of enjoyed it."

"Yeah?"

Nick nods, and I reach up to stroke his face. My fingers catch slightly on stubble, and I love the rough abrasion against them. I can almost feel the turn in my body as I realize how attracted I am to Nick.

"Would you like to go to dinner with me this week?" I ask.

"Are you asking me out on a date?"

"I am. I want to spend more time with you and get to know you better because I think there might be something here between us. I want to find out if I'm right."

Even in the dim light, Nick's smile illuminates his face. "I'd like that," he says, and then he slays me by saying, "I don't think I've ever been asked out on a real date before."

"I'm happy to change that," I say and lean in for another kiss.

Eleven

Nick

"I'm going on a date."

Roman's silence on the other side of the call speaks volumes.

After Aaron left—reluctantly on both our parts, but he wanted to make sure Kit was okay—I checked my phone and saw that Roman had done the same for me, texting that they wanted to see how I was doing. As soon as the call connected, I blurted that I'd been asked out before saying hello.

"With Aaron?" Roman finally asks.

"Yeah."

"I'm assuming he asked you."

"Why would you assume that?"

"Because you've never asked anyone on a date in your life."

"Yeah. Well. No one's exactly asked me either."

"You mean Julie didn't ask you out?" Roman asks, naming my first girlfriend.

I roll my eyes even though they can't see me. "Not really. We were on that ski trip, and things kind of...happened."

"Of course, they did," Roman says with a laugh. "Only you could have as many notches in your bedpost and not have asked someone out ever."

"Or gone on a real date. I mean, I've done stuff with people, gone to concerts and movies, gotten drinks or dinner with someone I was seeing, stuff like that, but, not like a real getting-to-know-you date with someone

I haven't fucked." I can feel Roman wince at my language even without seeing them. "Sorry."

"You like him," Roman says with the directness I love about them.

I'm quiet for a moment thinking about having Aaron in my place this afternoon. After walking him to the door, I laid down on the couch where we'd been cuddling and checked my phone. I'd been disappointed not to see a message from Aaron even though he'd just left my place, and I'd immediately called Roman noticing as I waited for the call to connect that the cushion where Aaron had rested his head still smelled like him.

Actually—I double-check—it kind of smells like both of us, and I like the way our scents combine to create something that's made of both of us. And then I roll my eyes at the sappiness of the thought.

"Yeah," I say. "I like him."

Roman makes a noise that's halfway between a chuckle and a hum of approval.

"What?" I ask.

"Nothing," they say. "Just...Kit, Aaron's friend, made a comment after you guys left the restaurant."

"I'm sure he did."

"It wasn't anything bad, just insinuating that you guys were hot for each other and couldn't wait. Dan lit into him. I swear, if looks could kill, we'd be holding a funeral for Dan."

"Kit's a bit of a drama queen, in case you couldn't tell."

"Oh, that was very obvious, trust me. Kit is definitely not short for 'kitten' no matter how many times he calls everyone 'sweetheart' or bats his lashes. And you know how guys like that rub Dan the wrong way."

I laugh, then sober. "You know it wasn't like that, right? With Aaron and me. We came back to my place because the group stirred up some memories for him. He's having a hard time with Zack's death."

"But something did happen or else you wouldn't be going out on a date."

For the first time in my life, I find myself wanting to keep those details to myself. And it's not because I'm embarrassed that all we did was kiss. There was no *all* about it. Kissing Aaron was everything, and it was wonderful. "It's not what you think," I say. "At least, not what my history would lead you to expect."

Silence from Roman's end greets my admission.

"What are you thinking?" I ask.

"I'm thinking Ty might have been right. Maybe you are looking for more than a physical relationship with Aaron."

"Maybe."

"I'm not trying to get you to tell me what you did do, but I will say, you've always wondered why I like cuddling and kissing but don't need sex. Forgive me if I hazard a guess that you might have figured it out a bit this afternoon."

I know the smile that crosses my face comes through in my voice when I say, "You might be right."

An hour before I'm supposed to meet Aaron for our date, I FaceTime Min in desperation. "I'm going on a date, and I've got no idea what to wear," I say as soon as she answers.

"You're what?"

"I know. Can we deal with that later? Right now, I need help figuring out what to wear, or I'm going to be late."

"You're serious."

"I am. And I need your help."

"Why? You go out all the time."

I swear, I love my friends, but sometimes I wish they could focus on what's most important. "I go to clubs and bars," I say. "Not dates."

"Wait," Min says. "Is this like a real date?" She gasps. "Is it with that hot guy who was at brunch?"

"Yes, it's a real date, and yes, it's with Aaron. Again, can we deal with that after you help me figure out what to wear?"

"Hunh."

"Miiiiiin," I whine.

"Niiiiick," she whines back. "This is big news. But, okay. Clothes first, teasing later. Do you know what you're going to be doing?"

"We're going for dinner at Elements and then drinks at Bourbon and Branch."

"Oooooo. Fancy. Okay, let's see what you've got."

I touch the button on my phone's screen to activate the rear camera so Min can see my closet.

"All right," she says after asking me to pull out a couple of options. "I'm thinking those navy pleated pants with a tobacco brown leather belt and matching shoes. On top...show me what you've got for shirts."

It literally takes Min five minutes to put together an outfit that has me looking like I'm walking a runway instead of being an aging college student, and I'm incredibly grateful.

"Now, tell me about this date," she says as I switch it back to a voice call so I can get changed.

"It hasn't happened yet," I say, but I'm grinning.

"Fair enough. How about the guy? How long has this been going on?"

"It hasn't. This is our first date."

"Hmmmm. Not willing to dish, playing coy...Nicholas Adler, do you have a boyfriend?"

She happens to ask me this question while I'm standing in front of the mirror, and I watch the color rise on my cheeks. God. I am already in so much trouble with Aaron. Instead of answering her, I say I need to get going so I'm not late.

"I want updates, young man," she says before telling me she loves me and hopes I have a great evening.

I take Lyft to the restaurant and arrive about ten minutes early, but Aaron's already waiting for me at the bar. He smiles as I slide onto the seat next to him, and I can't help leaning over and giving him a quick kiss.

"Looks like we were both eager," he says. "I like that."

The bartender comes over, and I order a dirty vodka martini, extra dirty. Aaron's already got a tumbler full of something that turns out to be an Old Fashioned. When my drink arrives, I lift my glass, and he does the same.

"To first dates," I say.

"To *successful* first dates," Aaron amends, and I take a quick gulp of my drink after we touch our glasses together.

"I'm really nervous," I admit with a shaky laugh.

Aaron bumps his shoulder against mine, then lays his hand on the bar close enough to mine that our little fingers touch. I roll my hand over in invitation, and Aaron accepts. His fingers are cold from his glass, but I feel the heat return to them as we touch.

"I am, too," he says. "Which is weird because it's not like we're complete strangers."

"I know." I shift on the seat so I can see his face better, but don't let go of his hand. "I had to get Min to help me choose my outfit."

Aaron laughs. "I got Kit to do the same. I will never hear the end of it." We both laugh, but then Aaron sobers. "Maybe we're nervous because tonight feels important to us."

Swallowing hard, I nod. He's right. It does. I've never been out with someone who makes me feel lightheaded and bubbly, twists my stomach in knots, and sends tiny shocks running through my body. And it's all because I'm sitting next to him, and we're holding hands, and he's looking at me like I'm the only person in the room.

"It does feel important," I whisper. "I don't want to screw things up, but, I'm being honest when I say I've never felt like this before when I'm with someone. It scares me."

The smile Aaron gives me is glorious. "I believe you," he says. "And it scares me, too, but in a good way."

I'm saved from having to respond by the hostess arriving to let us know our table is ready. We follow her through the dimly lit restaurant to a secluded table at the back of the dining room. A red rose graces one of the plates, and the butterflies in my stomach turn into pterodactyls as Aaron directs me to that side of the table and pulls out the chair for me.

"Wow," I say after the hostess gives us our menus and departs. "Did you ask for this?"

If the lighting weren't so low, I'd know for sure, but I think Aaron blushes. "I wanted everything to be perfect."

"No one's ever given me flowers," I say.

"I'm happy to be your first," Aaron replies. "Again."

His eyes sparkle, but it might only be the reflection from the candle on the table. I pick up the menu and busy myself perusing my choices. At least I would be if Aaron weren't so distracting. After a few moments, I pick up my head and find him staring at me, his menu still closed on his plate.

"Do you know what you're getting?" I ask.

"I've got a good idea," he says without taking his gaze from my face.

Now, it's my turn to blush. I glance down at my menu, then back at Aaron. "To eat," I say, thankful that the lighting is so low because it means there's hope Aaron won't be able to see how red my face has gotten. "Here. At the restaurant. For dinner."

Aaron laughs. "You're too easy."

"So, I've heard."

The smile on Aaron's face fades. He reaches out and takes hold of my hand. "Hey," he says. "I want you to know, I don't see you like your friends do. Whatever you've done in your past, it doesn't matter to me. What matters is what we have right here, right now, what we're exploring."

I nod, not trusting my voice to stay steady if I try to speak. Aaron makes me feel complicated things that have me questioning assumptions I've made about myself and what I want. Even the rose on my plate makes me ask why my heart beat harder when I saw it. That's never happened before. Romantic gestures usually send me running for the door. And the way Aaron held my chair for me. For fuck's sake. I nearly swooned. I don't know why Aaron makes me feel this way, or why I like it so much, but I do know that I don't want it to go away.

To be honest, I'm so distracted by the fact that Aaron is still holding my hand that I can't concentrate on the menu. I scan it quickly, find a pasta dish that sounds really good, then change my mind when our server lists pan-seared divers scallops with brown butter and capers. Aaron opts for the chicken piccata and suggests we split the baked brie with roasted figs as an appetizer, and I agree.

"Do you want wine?" he asks.

I still have about half my martini left, but I tell him wine would be great. He confers with the server, selects a moderately priced California pinot grigio, and then gives me his undivided attention as our date begins for real.

Twelve

Aaron

"HAVE YOU BEEN HERE before?" I ask as Nick settles next to me in our booth at Bourbon and Branch. The booths are narrow with straight backs, and Nick chooses to sit next to me, so we end up pressed together.

We're both rather full from dinner, but the walk from Elements to the speakeasy helped make room for one of their delicious cocktails. Plus, I'm not gonna lie, even if it hadn't, having my thigh pressed against Nick's is much better than having a table between us. If dinner had given me a wonderful opportunity to watch his gorgeous and expressive face as we talked through our meal and dessert, now I get to feel him next to me, and that's even better.

"I've never been here. It's really cool."

"Another first for me," I say and nudge Nick's shoulder. I want him to put his arm around me and bring our bodies closer together. It's ridiculous how much I crave that contact with him, and judging by the way he leans against me, the feeling is mutual. There's also the way his gaze keeps dropping to my mouth then back to my eyes. When our drinks arrive, I make a show of taking my first sip and licking my lips, smiling as I watch the heat build in Nick's expression.

The drinks here are strong and absolutely delicious and halfway through mine, I'm able to give voice to the thought that's been at the forefront of my mind since we sat down.

"Will you come home with me?" I ask. Concern clouds Nick's features, so I quickly add, "No pressure. I'm just not ready for our night to be over."

Nick studies my face, and I try to keep my expression neutral while my insides are a tangle of anticipation and hope. After a moment that seems to stretch for hours, Nick leans closer. I'm drawn forward, reducing the distance between us to almost nothing.

"I'd love to," he says against my mouth just before he kisses me.

We stay for another round because my place is literally right around the corner, a fact that Nick finds funny as we walk the short distance from the bar to my apartment.

"Were you planning this?" he asks as we take the elevator to the third floor.

"Would you think less of me if I had been?"

Nick crowds me against the back wall, presses a knee between my legs, and leans his body against mine. My heart races as I stare into his bright, blue eyes, barely hearing him tell me he finds confidence sexy as his lips skate along the line of my jaw.

It's on the tip of my tongue to tell him it wasn't my sureness at the outcome of this evening that led me to choose locations I could walk to, it was the readiness of escape if this date went the way so many of my previous ones had. I don't get the chance. Nick kisses me as the doors to the elevator open on my floor, and I get the barest of tastes as his tongue flicks over my lips before the doors start to close.

We break apart, Nick lunging for the doors, me for the button to make them open again. We're laughing as we exit the elevator. I take hold of Nick's hand and lead him down the hall. Every step we take feels new to me, as if I've never walked this hall before, never seen my own door, used my key, stepped across my threshold, heard my front door close and the lock engage. Nick's presence remakes the world, and his touch when he raises his hand to my face remakes me.

I rest my forehead against his, sharing space, sharing breath, but before I can say anything, Nick speaks.

"I'm not making any assumptions here," he says. "I'm not thinking that just because you invited me over, it means we're going to do anything more than talk." He smiles. "But I hope it does."

"I'm not making any assumptions either," I say. "I know you're used to things moving pretty fast, but that usually doesn't work for me." It's my turn to smile. "But, for the record, I wouldn't mind if they do."

"That's good to know," Nick says, and then we are kissing again.

Fuck. I love the way Nick kisses. It's possessive without being demanding, firm and confident without being aggressive. His hands cup my face, fingers tangling in my hair, thumbs stroking along my jaw, encouraging me to open and invite him in so we can taste each other. His every move asks permission, and I can't help but grant it as my senses become overwhelmed by him.

When my back touches the wall, I groan because it's brought Nick's body flush against mine. He's as hard as I am, and the feel of him rocking his hips against me sends shivers throughout my body. I am as turned on as I can ever remember being and can't stop myself from burrowing my hands beneath his jacket—we haven't even taken our coats off—then pulling his shirt from his pants so I can finally touch his bare skin.

I run my hands up the broad expanse of his back, tracing the lines of muscles and bone with my fingertips, then pressing my palms against the small of his back to bring him closer.

This time, it's Nick groaning into my mouth as his hips stutter forward, quick motions that make me long to know what it will feel like to have him in my bed. I have no doubts that's where we will end up, but despite my obvious desire, I am perfectly content to stay right where we are.

At least I am until Nick begins kissing along my jawline and down my neck, his hands dropping to my shoulders and pushing my jacket down my arms. I let it fall to the floor as Nick pauses, hands hovering over the button at my throat.

"Is this all right?" he asks.

I nod and gasp as his mouth returns to my neck, his fingers begin undoing the buttons on my shirt with deft movements. Cool air touches my chest as Nick opens my shirt enough that he can slip his hands inside. An embarrassing whimper escapes me as his warm hands touch my skin.

"Fuck, Aaron," he says, fingers skating over my ribs. "I want to see you."

For a moment, anxiety flares in my chest as I think about all the guys I've disappointed, but then my cock throbs, and I realize, yeah, I want that too. I want Nick more than I've ever wanted anyone, and that desire overrides any trepidation I might have about not being enough for him.

"Couch or bed?" I ask him.

He pulls away from me, his cautious gaze scanning my expression. "Whatever you want," he says. "Wherever you feel most comfortable."

I smile at his answer and kiss him. "Bed," I say with a confidence I've never felt before. "I want to see you, too."

Taking Nick by the hand, I lead him through the living room and up the stairs. He follows me without comment or hesitation. We pass through the loft space where I have my office and into the bedroom beyond.

I pause in the doorway, a last flare of anxiety making my heart race. Nick must see the panic in my expression because he takes a step back and asks if I'm okay.

"We don't have to do this," he says.

Taking a deep breath, I nod. "I know, but I want to." I draw him back to me, the feel of his body against mine settling something in me, helping me realize it's not fear or worry that's causing my reaction. It's anticipation. I draw Nick forward again.

Passing through the doorway, I turn on the lights but dim them. My room isn't as posh as Nick's. There are no pillows on my bed except the ones I sleep on, no plush comforter, no art on the walls. It's a utilitarian space meant for sleeping. I doubt Nick notices, though, as he crowds against my back, lips kissing my neck, hands never leaving my chest even as we move toward the bed.

When my knees touch the mattress, I lean back against Nick. He wastes no time taking advantage of this position, trailing his lips and tongue along the rigid line of tendons on the side of my neck while his hands caress their way upward until he slips my shirt over my shoulders and down my arms. I turn so I can do the same to him, admiring the smooth skin as I trace my way up from his fingers to his shoulders then back down over his lightly furred chest. I rest my hands lightly on his hips, thumbs brushing over the indents that mark the edges of firm muscles.

"You're gorgeous," I say, my face heating as I realize I've said it out loud.

Nick smiles. "You're not so bad yourself."

Then we are kissing again.

I am completely besotted by Nick, my entire focus on the sensations he causes in my body, the pleasure his touch gives me, and my desire to do the same for him. We kiss while exploring the expanse of skin in front of us.

Surprisingly, I am the one who asks if I can undo the button on Nick's pants, and he is the one who hesitates. I understand his trepidation immediately.

"For the record," I say, my voice husky and low. "I don't care. It doesn't have to lead to anything else. I just want to see and touch all of you."

Nick bites his lip, unsure, debating. Feeling bold, I press the palm of my hand against the bulge in his pants, smiling as Nick's eyelids flutter and his lips part. A sigh escapes his mouth.

"Whatever we do tonight, it will be perfect," I say. "I'm not judging you or putting pressure on you." I squeeze the hard ridge under my hand. It's a light touch, but it makes Nick gasp, and I grin, feeling playful, wicked. I lean in, my mouth against Nick's ear, and growl, "At least not much."

When I pull back, Nick's eyes are full of heat and desire. He moves into my space, then turns me, and we tumble onto my bed, our legs tangling together, mouths joined. I rut against Nick's thigh, my hands firm on his hips to hold him in place. I moan against his mouth at the sweet friction.

"Please?" I whisper, not really sure what I'm asking for but trusting I will love whatever Nick chooses to do in response.

"What do you want, Aaron?"

I go still and stare at him, silently begging him to decide for me. Continue kissing me, strip the rest of my clothes from my body, torment me with caresses, I don't care. I just don't want to say anything out loud and risk sounding like I lack the sexual imagination to keep him interested. But, Nick doesn't let me get away with not choosing.

"I won't do anything until you tell me what you want," he says, and I groan in frustration. "What's wrong?" he asks, but I shake my head. "Aaron?" There's true concern in his voice now. "Have I crossed a line? Do you want me to stop?"

Fuck. My insecurities are going to ruin everything. "No," I finally manage.

"Then what?" His gaze searches my face, and I see the moment he understands. He cups my face in his hand, his thumb gently moving back and forth over my cheek. "You want me to take control, is that it?"

I nod, relieved.

"No," he says. "Maybe once we know each other better, when I know where your boundaries are, but not tonight. This is too new, and I don't want to risk doing something you don't like or want." He leans down to kiss me. "You won't disappoint me, I promise," he whispers against my mouth, then kisses me again. "Now tell me what you want." He presses his thigh against my cock, and I groan.

"To be naked with you," I say.

He kisses me again. "Okay."

Without further ado, he undoes the button on my waistband and lowers the zipper. Then he scoots off the bed, grabs hold of my pant legs and pulls them from my body.

"Done," he says as he tosses them to the side and moves to return to the bed.

"But what about you?" I ask.

Pausing with one knee on the bed, he smirks at me. "You said you wanted to be naked with me, and now you are."

I prop myself up on my elbows. "I'm still wearing my briefs, and you're still in your pants."

Nick nods. "That's true. I didn't finish the job, did I?" He leans over me and hooks his fingers into the elastic that still encircles my waist. "May I?"

"Only if you're going to get naked, too," I say.

"Deal."

Nick makes short work of removing the last article of clothing from my body, then peels his own pants and briefs off. I can finally see the cock that has been teasing me all night, and I am not disappointed.

"I want that in my mouth," I say, nodding at it.

"All you had to do was ask," Nick says.

He kneels on the bed and crawls toward me as I push myself back against the pillows. Stradling my legs, he keeps moving up my body until his thighs bracket my chest and his cock is just out of reach of my mouth. A bead of precum glistens on the tip, and I lift my head so I can get my first taste.

I hum as the sharpness touches my tongue and lift my gaze, staring into Nick's eyes as I open my mouth and take him inside. Nick's eyelids close, and he takes a deep breath, a sigh escaping from between his lips that turns into a guttural moan as I slide my lips down his shaft, my tongue teasing and caressing his length as I descend.

"Fuck, Aaron," he says as he exhales.

His hips rock forward gently, pushing his cock deeper into my mouth, and God, I love how perfect he is. I love that he's careful. I love that he hasn't immediately jammed himself as deep as he can get. I love that he's letting me take my time to explore the feel of him in my mouth, to find my own pleasure in the act.

With my gaze still fixed on his, I ease off then take him deep. My tongue swirls around his hard cock, finding ridges and veins to trace and tease. This time, when I pull back, I leave the soft tip resting against my lips, teasing at his slit with my tongue. There's more precum, and I lap it up before taking him all the way to the back of my throat in one movement.

Nick hisses, but his hips rock forward as he begins to thrust lightly between my lips. I pause and let him control the slide and force, encouraging him to go harder with my moans. I'm not usually a fan of having my face fucked, but with Nick, I want it. I want him to use me, to find his own pleasure and let me find my own in the act.

With a groan, Nick moves away, but I don't have time to feel bereft before he's laying his body on top of me, his mouth finding mine, humming as he tastes himself on my tongue. Our hips move together, cocks brushing, and the friction is exquisite. Propping himself up on his elbows, Nick thrusts harder against me, and I arch my back to meet him. I wrap my legs around his, wanting to keep him close, to keep us connected, and lower my hand to take hold of both our cocks.

We're both breathing hard but unwilling to stop kissing. It's sloppy and uncoordinated, spit runs down my chin, but I don't care. My entire body is alive, and I'm flying. Sex has never felt like this with anyone else, and before I'm ready for it to be over, I'm on the edge.

"Shit, Nick," I breathe against his lips. "I'm close."

"So, am I."

His hips jut forward, and I close my hand tighter around our cocks. He does it again, thrusting hard against mine, and then again. My whole body lights up, and I suddenly can't take the feel of his tongue in my mouth. It's too much. I pitch my head back, throat exposed, and Nick nips at the tender skin under my jaw. The tiny bite of pain sends me over the edge, my orgasm hitting on a silent, open-mouthed scream that leaves me gasping for breath as it radiates through my body.

Nick follows me over, frantically thrusting into my cum-slicked fist until his body goes rigid. I stare up at him, watching the flush that rises up his chest to his throat, the tension in his jaw, and the shudders that rack his body as his climax takes control. He gasps, drags in a deep breath, and collapses on top of me.

I wrap him in my arms, place gentle kisses on his lips and cheeks, the sound of our harsh breaths echoing in my bedroom. As our breathing returns to normal, I trace Nick's face with my fingers, memorizing his features. His eyebrows, the bridge of his nose, the outline of his lips, the line of his jaw, the intricate whorls of an ear, the sweat-dampened strands of hair at his temple. I want to remember them all, to keep this moment indelible in my memory.

But, of course, the moment fades. Nick hasn't moved off me, and I shift beneath him, worried that I'm taking too long to recover, anticipating his excuses for why he needs to leave, aware of the cooling cum growing sticky and uncomfortable between our bodies.

"Are you okay?" Nick asks, lifting his head so he can see my face.

I can't look him in the eye. "Yeah."

"Aaron." His tone is quiet but firm, and I let my gaze drift to his. "Are you okay?"

Nodding, I feel tears well in the corners of my eyes and blink to try to clear them. Nick rolls to the side, then uses his fingers to gently wipe away the tears, which only makes more of them appear.

"I'm sorry," I say. "I don't know why I'm crying."

Instead of turning away, Nick wraps me in his arms, holding me as I fall apart. His hands trace circles on my back, and he makes quiet, comforting sounds until I calm.

With an embarrassed laugh, I pull away, sit up and wipe at the lingering moisture with the back of my hand. Nick sits up as well, but he doesn't move away from me. Instead, he turns and straddles my lap, cupping my face between his palms to make me look at him again. He gives me soft kisses until I sigh against his mouth as my emotions settle.

"That was mortifying," I say.

Nick shakes his head. "That was honest." He kisses me. "And brave." Another kiss. "And strong."

"I don't feel brave or strong," I say. "I just broke down in front of a guy I really like, who made me come harder than I ever have in my life. I want to feel attractive and sexy."

With his fingers beneath my chin, he lifts my head and gives me another kiss. Nick takes his time with this one. The soft press of his lips gives way to a tease of his tongue. He presses his thumb lightly against the hinge of my jaw, and I open for him, but his exploration of my mouth is a slow, sensual glide of his tongue along mine, a sweet tango in which the goal is to find a mutual rhythm rather than dominance. I love it. And I love how Nick seems to be giving this kiss his full attention.

When we part, Nick runs his fingers along my cheeks and smiles. "Did that convince you that I think you're sexy and attractive?"

I nod. "Yeah."

"Good. And for the record, I really like you, too."

Wrapping my hands around his waist, we rock against each other for a bit. "Stay?" I ask him.

"I'd love to."

Thirteen

Nick

I wake in the morning to the sound of a phone ringing and reach my hand to where my nightstand should be. I'm confused because I can't find it, but my mind doesn't catch up to where I actually am until I hear Aaron answer the call.

"Hey, mom, what's up?" he says as I roll over to face him.

Even though we haven't known each other for long, I hear the wariness in Aaron's voice. From what he's told me, any time his parents call it's to talk about Zack, or how the investigation into his murder is going nowhere. They want him to do something, but there's nothing to do.

"You're kidding?" Aaron says, and I watch his expression change from guarded to hopeful. "That's amazing. Have they been able to get any prints?"

I can literally feel the way Aaron's body hums with excitement as the conversation continues. Obviously, it's good news, like a break in the case at last. Wanting to give Aaron privacy, I roll over intending to get out of bed, find my clothes, and head home. I've got work that needs to get done, and a meeting to prepare for this afternoon with the head of my department about our upcoming system update.

My feet have just touched the floor when Aaron puts his hand on my shoulder. I turn to look at him, and he shakes his head, mouths the word "stay." I raise my eyebrows asking if he's sure, and he nods. So, I get back under the covers and snuggle up next to him. He puts his arm around me, and I slide mine across his waist.

I have never done something like this before. Never cuddled with a sex partner except in the afterglow of a good orgasm, never had a partner ask me to be part of such an intimate moment of their life. It feels nice that Aaron asked me to stay, and I relax against him, my fingers gently stroking his stomach and playing with his treasure trail.

As I listen to Aaron speak to his mom, feeling the rumble of his voice in his chest, I realize it's not so much that I've never done this before, it's also that I've never *wanted* to. I've wanted my relationships to remain simple and unencumbered, kept boundaries on how much time I spend with my partners, got bored and twitchy whenever they asked for more. That's the primary reason I gravitated almost exclusively to hookups after the disaster with Lauren. They were just easier.

And then I met Aaron.

Maybe this thing between us grew organically because I wasn't sizing him up as a potential partner when we met. Maybe that gave me time to get to know Aaron before I realized I was attracted to him. I'm not sure. Because I did notice how attractive he was the moment I walked into the coffee shop to tell him I'd been with Zack the night he was killed, but I was still reeling from my failure with Zack and not looking for anyone at that point.

"Okay," Aaron says, and I pick my head up. "Yeah. That sounds great. I'll see you then."

Aaron ends the call and tosses his phone onto the nightstand then turns to me and wraps me in his arms.

"Good news?" I ask.

"Finally." Aaron's smile is brilliant. "They found Zack's phone and wallet."

"That's amazing," I say.

"It is. And the best part is that they got a partial print off the wallet." He rests his forehead against mine and closes his eyes. "We might get justice after all."

"I'm really happy for you. That must be such a relief after all this time."

He nods. "Like you wouldn't believe. My mom wants everyone over at the house tonight for dinner."

"That's great," I say, feeling strangely disappointed that I won't be able to see Aaron later that night.

"Hey. Why don't you come with me? I'd love to introduce you to my family. I mean, you're part of the reason the police were able to find the wallet and phone."

"I am?"

"They were behind a dumpster down the street from your place. Without knowing where Zack had been, the police wouldn't have known where to look. And that's all thanks to you."

Aaron kisses me, and I feel all my reasons for saying no to his invitation crumbling to dust.

"Okay," I say even as my stomach clenches with anxiety. But then I see how happy Aaron is that I've said yes, and I figure my discomfort is a small price to pay for seeing his incredible smile.

Aaron's parents live on the Peninsula about half an hour—without traffic—south of San Francisco in Millbrae, which means Aaron arrives at my place around six to pick me up. I'm waiting in front of my building and only a little surprised to see the passenger side door open and a disgruntled Kit emerge. He bows to me and motions for me to get into the car.

"I guess I know who the favored child is," Kit pouts as he opens the back door and gets in.

"I can sit in the back," I say.

"You're fine, he's just being a brat," Aaron tells me and looks over his shoulder where Kit is making a show of putting on his seatbelt. "Do you need a timeout or something?"

Kit sticks his tongue out at Aaron, then becomes absorbed in his phone.

I settle into the seat beside Aaron and immediately lean towards him to kiss him but then hesitate.

With an amused smile, Aaron closes the distance between us and kisses me. "Hi," he says.

"Hi," I say, unreasonably breathless as a grin breaks across my face.

"O.M.G.," Kit intones dramatically from the backseat. "It's like watching my grandparents kiss. Ew."

"Aren't I younger than you?" I ask.

Kit fixes me with a glare. "Youth is a state of mind."

Both Aaron and I roll our eyes, and Aaron mouths a silent apology at me.

"I saw that," Kit says, though it's highly unlikely because he's back to staring at his phone.

The drive south passes without further comment from Kit beyond the clicking of his fingers on his screen. Gradually, Aaron and I start talking about how we spent the rest of our day. It's nothing exciting—I worked, he cleaned and did laundry—but I get a warm feeling in my chest hearing these small details of Aaron's life.

We get off the freeway at the Millbrae exit, and Aaron wends his way through suburban side streets named for trees until he pulls up in front of a sand-colored Spanish colonial house with a small but beautifully landscaped yard.

"I cannot believe this is where we grew up," Kit grumbles as he exits the car, reminding me that he and Zack have been friends since kindergarten.

"Which was your house?" I ask.

He points across the street at a house that is nearly identical to Aaron's except that it's painted a rich terracotta. "My parents sold when the market was at its peak and moved to the Oregon coast," he says and stalks his way up the front path.

"What's going on with him?" I ask Aaron.

Shrugging, Aaron says, "I don't know. I keep thinking it's Zack's death, but now I'm starting to think there's something else. He's not usually this..."

"Bitchy?" I suggest.

"Yeah. I was trying to find a nicer way to say it, though." He takes hold of my hand and entwines our fingers. "Let's go see my parents."

I raise our joined hands. "Are they going to be okay with this when you tell them who I am?"

"I don't know." Aaron lifts our hands to his mouth and kisses the back of mine. "But they're going to find out eventually, so it might as well be today when we've got good news."

"Okay."

I let Aaron lead the way, following Kit's path from the street to the house and then inside where I immediately hear the sound of several voices. Aaron's family. I'd be lying if I said I wasn't nervous. There haven't been too many opportunities to meet parents in my history, so this is new territory for me, not to mention the added issue of being some random guy Zack hooked up with the day he died who is now dating Zack's older brother.

As if sensing my growing nerves, Aaron squeezes my hand as he leads me through a living room immaculately decorated in shades of white and beige accented with olive green.

"As soon as Zack and I moved out, Mom went nuts with redecorating the house," he says. "While we were growing up, it was a lot less..."

"Stark?" I ask.

He laughs. "Yeah. Zack had a ton of friends who were always over here, and it showed, especially downstairs where our rooms were."

"Am I gonna get to see your childhood bedroom, Aaron?" I tease and grin when he turns to give me a sly smile.

"Maybe," he says with a wink.

We follow a hallway to the back of the house and cross through a doorway into a gathering of about half a dozen people. There are two older couples, but since one has already corralled Kit, I make a guess that the other couple is Aaron's parents. It helps that Aaron looks a lot like his dad. There's also a woman who looks like she's around the same age as Aaron, and I assume that's his sister. She's standing next to a guy who's got his arm around her. So I'm guessing that's her husband. There's also a couple of younger guys standing next to Kit. They all give me a once-over as soon as we step into the space, which leads me to believe Kit has filled them in on who I am and that these are Zack's friends.

The woman I surmised is Aaron's mother sees him and cries out then rushes to wrap him up in her arms. I stand to the side while they embrace, not sure whether I should introduce myself or wait until Aaron can do it, but the older man steps forward and holds out his hand.

"I'm Robert, Aaron's father."

I shake his hand. "Nick," I say. "It's nice to meet you." Before I can figure out what to add to that, Kit snorts loudly. The sound gets Aaron's attention, and he looks over at me and his dad.

"Nick's the reason the police knew where to search in Hayes Valley," he says.

"He's also the reason Zack was in Hayes Valley in the first place," Kit says.

The tension in the kitchen increases tenfold, and I look for an escape, but Aaron walks over, puts his arm around me, pulls me close, and kisses my temple, then looks across the kitchen. “Kit.” His voice is low, but the warning is clear.

“What, *Aaron*? Forgive me for thinking you could have done better than falling for one of Zack’s leftovers.” He turns his head to take in everyone in the room. “Or has no one noticed that they’re together?”

Aaron’s mother gasps, but I can’t tell if it’s because of the way Kit’s behaving or because of what he said. One of Kit’s friends leans forward and whispers something in his ear, another steps to his side and slings an arm around Kit’s shoulders. I’m distracted from watching the interaction by Aaron’s mother coming up to me and pulling me into her arms.

I’m shocked speechless, and it takes me a moment to relax. When she lets me go and steps back, she wipes her eyes.

“Thank you,” she says. “I am so grateful you came forward.” She laughs. “I’m sorry. I’m Helen. This is Shayna, Aaron and Zack’s sister, and her husband, Mark.” She continues around the room, introducing everyone to me including Zack’s friends and the other couple who turn out to be the parents of one of the guys.

Everyone echoes Helen’s thanks for helping with the investigation. Everyone except Kit, of course, who stands rigidly in the corner, glaring at me, and it suddenly hits me what’s going on. Aaron thought Kit had a thing for Zack, but I think, given how he’s acting toward me, it’s a lot more likely that Kit has a bad case of unrequited love for *Aaron*. I’m not going to say anything because it’s just a hunch, but I’m definitely going to ask one of my friends to help me navigate this unexpected wrinkle if Aaron’s going to be a part of my life. Which I really hope he will be.

Conversation gradually resumes around us. Shayna and her husband join our circle, and Aaron doesn’t leave my side as we talk to his parents about how new and unexpected our relationship is, and how we're just figuring things out.

"Last night was actually our first date," he says, then gives me a lopsided, hopeful smile. "So, I guess this might be our second?"

Weirdest second date ever, I think, but I nod. "It could be," I say, and Aaron's smile becomes genuine.

After Kit's friends pull him out the French doors and onto the deck, Aaron tells his parents and the other couple about me rescuing Kit at the club last weekend. I notice Kit's friends pull out vapes, and it doesn't take long for a distinctive skunky odor to reach us.

"Jace is worried about him," the older woman, who was introduced to me as Ellen, says. Jace is her son and one of the guys currently standing outside with Kit.

"I am, too," Aaron says. "He's taken Zack's death really hard."

I don't say anything about my suspicion that there's more going on for Kit than that and idly cast my glance around the kitchen while the conversation turns to him. It's homey, but also immaculate with gleaming stainless steel appliances and pressed-quartz counters.

I'm oddly relaxed in the midst of this uber-domestic scene. Aaron has introduced me to his parents, and I haven't run screaming from the house. We haven't defined anything about our...well, I guess it is a relationship...haven't put a definite label on it, but I find myself wishing he could have introduced me as his boyfriend. It's an unfamiliar feeling, but as I stand next to Aaron, my arm wrapped around his waist, his arm around my shoulders, I have an inkling that this is something I could get used to having in my life. That *he* is someone I want to have in my life. And, somehow, that thought isn't one that makes me want to do anything other than snuggle closer to Aaron and wish we could be alone for a few minutes so I could tell him how grateful I am to him for seeming to want the same thing.

My thoughts are interrupted by Jace stepping back into the kitchen to announce that he and his friends are going to take Kit home. A silent conversation goes on between Jace and his mom that I can't interpret, but fifteen minutes later, Kit and the rest of Zack's friends are gone.

Aaron nudges me, and when I look at him, he asks if I want to see more of the house. There's an invitation in his eyes that I can't miss, so I say sure.

"I'm going to show Nick around," Aaron announces and leads me out of the kitchen and back to the hallway where stairs lead to the lower level. "My parents' bedroom is on the upper floor, but you probably don't want to see that."

"I don't know," I say. "I kind of have a kink about doing it in parents' beds." I grin at Aaron's shocked expression, then laugh so he knows I'm kidding. "I did it once when I was in high school, and it was just...weird. Not sexy at all. Especially when we found their stash of sex toys." I shudder. "Scarred for life. I still freak out when I see purple dildos."

Aaron finally laughs. "Good thing mine's black," he says and leaves me speechless as he heads down the stairs.

I follow him and take in the family photos that line both walls. The photos closest to the top of the stairs are of a baby and young child that has to be Aaron. When he's a toddler, he's joined by a sibling, and then, just after an adorable photo of him on his first day of preschool, he and Shayna are pictured holding a new baby, which is obviously Zack. From then on, it's the three kids, and I watch them all age from toddlers to elementary school kids to middle school. By the time Aaron's in high school, it's clear how similar he and Zack look. The stairs end in a family room and the far wall displays high school and college graduation photos of all three siblings.

Aaron doesn't say a word as I take them in. It's amazing how much alike Aaron and Zack look, almost like they're twins despite the obvious age difference. It's also disconcerting knowing I'm looking at the man I shared space with right before he died. The man I invited into my home without knowing anything about him, only caring that he wanted my dick. I didn't even know his name until I met his brother. God. I am such a piece of shit.

"Hey," Aaron says softly as he wraps me in his arms and wipes at the tears I didn't even realize were running down my cheeks. "Whatever it is, it's okay."

I shake my head and bury my face in his shoulder. I don't want to look at him. I don't want to see echoes of Zack in his features. Not right now.

"I'm sorry," I mumble.

"Nothing to be sorry about." He rocks me gently against his body. "I know you didn't really know him, but it's got to be a shock to see his pictures. *I'm* sorry I didn't think about how that would affect you before I asked if you wanted to come down here."

I lean back so I can see his face, and it stuns me that I'm not seeing Zack at all. I'm seeing Aaron. Only Aaron. The Zack I met was perfectly styled, his appearance sculpted and contoured by makeup and regular visits to the gym. I'd thought he was stunning in his profile pics, even more so when we met at my car. But that image can't hold a candle to the man standing in front of me. Aaron is beautiful and perfect, his gorgeous eyes full of concern for me.

In the short time I've known him, I've had so many firsts with Aaron. They're not the firsts I always thought were important, the ones I was told were important, the ones that meant I was a man and around which I based my sense of who I was. But now I know. These firsts I've had with him are the ones that truly matter.

And I know something else.

For the first time in my life, I'm falling for someone. And, from his expression, I think he might be falling for me, too.

Fourteen
Aaron

I'm not completely sure what's going on for Nick, but as soon as I see tears welling in his eyes, I can't help but wrap my arms around him and tell him it's okay. Beneath his cockiness and attempts at keeping up the libertine façade, I've seen his softer side. It's the part of him that made it impossible for him to stay silent when he realized what had happened to my brother, the part that wouldn't let Kit stay in a dangerous situation, and the part that agreed to come with me to meet my family knowing it might cause issues.

And when he leans back and stares into my eyes, it's not lust I see in those incredible blue eyes. It's something deeper, something that takes my breath away when he closes the distance between us and presses his lips against mine. I taste the faintest hint of salt as I open to him and let him explore my mouth, but then it's gone, and my senses are filled with the wonder that is Nick. The scent of him as I inhale, the taste as we kiss, the feel of him in my arms.

He is everything I have ever wanted but never thought I'd find, and as we kiss in front of all those family photos, I can almost believe that bringing Nick into my life was Zack's final gift to me.

"Now you're crying," Nick says softly, his fingers brushing away the dampness that has spilled onto my cheeks. He rests his forehead against mine. "Today was a lot, hunh?"

I let out a huge breath and nod. "More than I thought it would be. Thank you for coming with me."

"Of course," he says, and the tone of his voice makes me believe that he truly understands how much it means to me to have him here.

"I think I'm about ready to leave," I say, suddenly tired and wishing to be alone with Nick. I want quiet cuddles and soft kisses while a movie we've lost interest in plays in the background, and I'm reminded that Nick's apartment actually has a fireplace. "Can we go back to your place?"

The smile Nick gives me is radiant. "Of course. I wanted to ask, but I wasn't sure..."

I kiss him and tell him what I'm thinking.

"That sounds amazing," he says. He turns his head and looks at the closed doors to what used to be Zack's room and mine. "We'll leave the childhood bedroom fantasy for another time."

Laughing, I take his hand but pause before leading him up the stairs. "Zack's room is full of the stuff from his apartment. We'll have to go through it all at some point, but..." I shrug. "I have no idea when my parents are going to be ready to do that."

Nick leans against my side. "No sad thoughts about Zack," he says. "Today is a happy day. There's progress in the case. You and your family may get justice after all. Everything else can wait for another day."

I nod and swallow. "Yeah."

WE AREN'T ABLE TO get out of my parents' house for another hour because both my sister and mother decide to grill Nick. Everything from where he grew up to what he studied in school is fair game. I try to intervene a couple of times, try to redirect them to other topics, but Nick seems to be holding his own and might actually be enjoying the impromptu inquisition if the sparkle in his eyes is anything to go by.

Eventually, I'm able to extricate him from their endless questions and get us both into my car with only a few storage containers of food my mother insisted we take.

"At least we have dinner sorted," Nick says as he puts the bag holding the food at his feet.

"Which will save us from being interrupted by a delivery person." I wink at him as I press the ignition button on my car and laugh at Nick's dumbfounded expression. I've never been one to tease the guys I've been with or make suggestive comments to them, but it's different with Nick. He makes me feel light and brings out a playful side of myself I hadn't known existed.

More than that, though, I know even if I'm the one who brought up having sex, Nick won't get upset with me if I don't get aroused or want to spend the evening kissing on the couch instead of fucking. He'll go at my speed, give me what I want when and how I want it.

I want to do the same for him, too. I want to take care of him and make sure his needs are met as well. I get the feeling that for all his friends see him as a Lothario, Nick's really a caretaker at heart. I also get the feeling he hasn't been able to show that side of himself that often.

"There's a couple of guest spaces in my building's garage," Nick says as I turn onto his street. "I'll get out to open the door, and you can pull into one of them."

After I park, Nick joins me, and we walk hand in hand to the elevator. Once inside, Nick faces me, presses me lightly against the wall, and kisses me until the bell dings to announce we've arrived on his floor.

"That ride wasn't nearly long enough," I complain as we exit.

Nick laughs. "You're right. Usually, I have more stamina."

We're still laughing when Nick opens his door, and we step into his apartment. I was here less than a week ago to deal with Kit, but it feels like I've never seen the place before. It's not the difference in lighting—Nick had kept the lights low for Kit's sake—but the difference in me. I take the bag with the food from Nick's hands and set it on the kitchen counter, then turn to him and walk him backwards until he's against the wall.

"Hi," I say.

"Hi." He smirks. "Probably should put the food in the refrigerator so it doesn't spoil."

"Probably," I say but don't move away from him.

"Do you want a beer?" he asks, his gaze rising to meet mine, then flicking down to my mouth.

"No."

"Wine?" His gaze follows the same trajectory, but this time his tongue darts out to run along his upper lip.

"No." I move in closer, my mouth just brushing his, our bodies touching only enough to be aware of each other. A tease that has my cock getting hard.

"Then I don't know what I have that you could possibly want."

"Don't sell yourself short," I say. "Use your imagination."

Nick hums, leans his head back until it rests against the wall, exposing his throat. He closes his eyes, and I can't resist the invitation.

I place gentle kisses just below his ear then continue to kiss and nip my way down his jawline. Sometimes I tease the soft skin under his chin with the tip of my tongue, sometimes I bite softly along the bone with my front teeth, and sometimes I let my lips map the contours of his neck.

The quiet sounds Nick makes—the hums, sighs, soft moans—coupled with the lazy way his hips rock against mine are driving me nuts. My blood fizzes with arousal, but I'm in no hurry to move on to anything else, and I love that Nick isn't trying to rush us to the couch or his bedroom. We'll get there. We both know that.

I let my hands take over for a bit, tracing Nick's cheekbones, dragging a fingernail along the perimeter of his plush mouth. I can't stop playing with the divot over his top lip, enamored with how soft his skin is there.

"Why is everything so easy with you?" I ask.

Nick's eyes open, and I see the same emotion in them I saw when we were holding each other at my parents' house. Not only can I see it in his expression, I feel it in my body. A warmth and weight that emanate from my core, grounding me, comforting me, connecting me to the beautiful man in front of me in ways I didn't think were possible. And that is when I know, as improbable as it might be, I'm falling in love with him.

He shakes his head, and for a moment, I think he's responding to my thoughts rather than what I said.

"I don't know," he whispers against my lips. "But it feels like that for me, too." His gaze finds mine. "You're the first person I've ever wanted to be with as much as I want to fuck. Maybe even more because I'm not thinking about anything but being able to touch you and kiss you. Talk to you. Be with you in any way I can."

My mouth touches his, and he opens for me, letting me explore and taste him. His hands slide under my jacket, but it's so he can put his arms around me and pull me against him, not to start undressing me. And, yeah, we're both hard, and the friction against my cock feels amazing, but it's because I'm with Nick.

We continue kissing for several minutes until we're both rocking against each other, our breath more gasps and moans than anything else. Nick steps away from me and shrugs out of his coat, and I do the same. His face is flushed, sweat beading at his hairline, and when I run my fingers through my own hair, I feel how damp it is.

Nick hangs up our coats, then puts the leftovers my mother gifted us in the fridge.

"Being a responsible adult," I tease.

"I try," he says, then grins. "Really, I needed a few moments to cool off."

"Good thinking." I step into the kitchen, put my hands on his hips and guide him backwards until his ass touches the counter.

"What do you want, Aaron?"

He asked me that question before, and I hadn't been able to answer in a way that wasn't about everyone else's needs. But tonight, I know exactly what to tell him because it's the truth.

"I want you to take me to your bed and make love with me."

Nick's eyes widen. I see the fear and uncertainty in them, and I think I know what he's worried about. Instead of reassuring him or telling him he's already shown me how generous a lover he could be, I lean in and kiss him, letting him know I don't care what we do as long as it involves being with him.

The kiss starts gentle with a soft pressing of lips, a tease of tongue. Nick's fingers pull my shirt from my waistband and find their way under the cloth to rest lightly on my back. I run mine through his hair, tilting his head back so I have more leverage. As far as passionate kisses go, I'm sure Nick has had hotter ones, but I'm not trying to outdo everyone he's ever been with. I only care about the here and now, who we are together, who we'll be going forward, and I try to put all that into the kiss. And then I feel it. Nick's body relaxes against mine. The tension that thrums through his muscles eases, and he becomes pliant in my arms.

His mouth opens wider, the pressure of his lips gets more insistent, his tongue tangles with mine, and his hands rise to my shoulders to press me closer. It's like he wants to erase all the space between us. When he whimpers then gasps, I'm done for. I break the kiss, panting hard, because I need to pause and catch my breath.

This time, when I pull back enough to see Nick's expression, it's full of wonder.

"All right," he says as if he's speaking the words for the first time. "Yeah. I want that, too."

Fear flashes through his expression, too quick for me to be fully certain except that I know what it is. And I also know that this may be the first time someone's wanted to make love rather than fuck.

"Let's go," I whisper, and Nick shivers beneath my hands.

"Yeah."

His word ghosts across my lips, but before I can lean in for another taste of him, he slips his hands from beneath my shirt and takes hold of my hand.

"Downstairs," he says and leads me out of the kitchen.

I follow willingly, more excited than I've ever been at the prospect of getting naked with a man.

Once we're inside Nick's bedroom, we pause to kiss again and remove clothing that's becoming more cumbersome and unnecessary by the minute. Shirts get untucked and unbuttoned, falling to the floor at our feet while we explore each other with our hands and mouths.

Nick puts his hand on the waistband of my jeans, breaking the kiss only long enough to ask, "Can I?"

"Yes," I breathe out. "And for you?"

"Absolutely."

Jeans get pushed down to the floor, and we grin like fools against each other's mouths as we try to remove them without breaking contact. As soon as I'm completely free, Nick drops to his knees.

I groan as he mouths me through my briefs, nuzzling at my balls until I can't stand it and pull the elastic waistband lower so he can free my cock. Then I'm enveloped by the wet heat of his mouth, and I'm in heaven. I can't recall anything feeling this good before.

I put my hands on Nick's head, not to control him, but to steady myself, and also because I need to touch him. His hair curls around my fingers, soft and silky. I let them rest there, but Nick has other ideas and begins bobbing his head, taking me deeper then pushing back into my hands, and I understand what he wants. My thrusts into his mouth get more forceful as I hold him in place, using his mouth as I want.

Tipping his head back gives me a better angle, and I thrust deep enough to make Nick's eyes water.

"Do you want me to stop?" I ask.

"Unh uh."

His voice vibrates around my cock, and I draw in a sharp breath, groaning as I fight the urge to feel his throat around my glans. Nick's hands are on my ass, though, pulling me deeper. His brilliant blue eyes stare up at me, urging me to let go, so I do. I thrust hard and deep, hitting the back of his throat every time I surge forward. He's taken almost all of me into his mouth, and one hand strokes the remaining bit while his other massages my balls. Tears leak from the corners of his eyes and spit from his mouth, but I can tell how much he's loving this from the fire in his expression as his tongue strokes and caresses my length.

And then he swallows around me.

With a shout, I pull out, grab the base of my cock and squeeze until I know I'm not going to come. I hoist Nick to his feet and kiss him, reveling in the bitter taste of my precum in his mouth.

While we kiss, Nick works my briefs over my ass and down my legs until they shimmy to the ground, and I step out of them. I do the same for him, and we both groan when our cocks finally touch. As much as I would love to keep doing this forever, I want him on the bed so I can explore his body more fully.

It takes a surprising amount of time to accomplish the short move from the doorway to the bed because we can't stop kissing. Eventually we're stretched out alongside each other, face to face, and I am finally able to touch him the way I want to, finally able to experience his hands on my body.

Still kissing, our hands roam and tease, caress and stroke. I tangle our legs together, and Nick rocks his hips together so our cocks can touch. We both moan.

"Do you want?" I ask with a gentle thrust forward, just enough for my cock to rub alongside his.

"I want," he says.

"I'm probably going to be tight. It's been a while."

Nick closes his eyes and takes a few deep breaths. "I'll try to go slow," he says.

And then we are moving. Nick reaches into a drawer and pulls out condoms and lube, I scoot up on the bed a bit. He grabs a pillow and puts it under my hips, then settles himself between my bent knees, leaning forward to kiss my mouth before trailing touches and kisses down my throat, across my chest and abs.

Gentle nips outline my hips, and then Nick's mouth is back on my cock, sucking gently as he opens the bottle of lube and gets some on his fingers. I tense at their first, cool touch, but Nick tells me it's okay, he'll take care of me.

"Tell me if it's too much, and I'll stop," he says as his fingers stroke the sensitive skin around my hole.

"It's good," I say. "Very good." My voice is nearly a purr as I push against his touch. When he finally breaches me, I gasp then moan. "More."

Slowly, so slowly I'm nearly crying, Nick presses inside me. One finger, then two, his thumb still stroking my taint, mouth caressing the length of my cock. When he adds a third finger, the tip of his tongue dives into my slit, and I cry out. It's time. I want him inside me. I want to feel us move together. I want to know how much pleasure we can give each other. And then, I want to fall asleep with Nick, wake up, and do it all again.

"I'm ready," I say.

"Okay."

Nick withdraws his fingers and wipes them on his thigh, then opens the condom. He hesitates.

"Are you okay?" I ask.

"Yeah." He blows out a breath. "Yeah. I'm good. Just...you know..."

Ah.

I roll up to my knees. "Everything we've done has been amazing," I say as I take his cock in hand. "You're amazing." I give him a good long downward stroke then pull back up and twist my fingers around his glans. "You won't disappoint me no matter what we do."

Bending down, I take his cock in my mouth, loving the burst of salt and bitter on my tongue. He's so hard the veins press against my tongue, and I caress each one.

"Oh, God, Aaron, stop."

I pull off, look up at Nick, and take the condom from his hand. Back on my knees, I unroll it down his length, then lie down and open up my arms. "I'm all yours," I say. "Come take me."

Nick smiles. He grabs the lube and puts some on the condom, then around my entrance. And then finally—finally!—he presses the blunt head of his cock to my hole.

Breathing out, I smile at him as the knot of muscle and nerves gives way. The stretch is intense, but it feels incredible. Once he's fully seated, he bends down and kisses me.

"You feel amazing," he says.

"Right back at ya," I say and rock my hips in a way that makes him groan.

Our soft and rhythmic thrusts slowly build in power and intensity. The incredible slide of Nick's cock makes me cry out over and over again, urging him on until I can't take it any longer. I take hold of myself, timing the movement of my hand with Nick's thrusts. He looks down, his eyes blazing, and tells me to keep going.

"Fuck, Aaron," he gasps.

"Yeah. Come on. With me."

As soon as I say that, my body tightens, all my senses focused on where Nick and I are joined, to my cock which pulses. One more stroke, and I am flying, the orgasm turning my vision white. I peak a second time, a burst of cum spilling over my hand, when Nick comes, his body stilling, mouth open but no sound emerging. He gazes at me, his eyes wild. And then he groans, gasps. I feel him fill the condom and sigh.

Every nerve in my body hums, and I welcome Nick into my arms as he lowers himself to my chest. I kiss his forehead. His arms wrap around me, and he turns his head so he can kiss my neck, my jaw, and finally my mouth.

We kiss for a long time, then get up and shower before falling back into bed again. Nick pulls the covers over us, snuggles into my arms, and sighs.

"I get it," he whispers.

"Get what?" I ask, my voice equally as quiet.

Nick ducks his head, hiding his expression from me, but I reach down and lift his chin, so he looks at me.

"Get what?" I repeat.

"What Ty's been talking about for the past year."

His cheeks turn red, and I decide to let him off the hook. But, yeah, I get it, too.

In that moment of drowsiness before I fall asleep, I think about Zack. There will always be a hole in my heart where my brother used to live, but I can't help thinking he had something to do with Nick and I finding each other. I kiss the top of Nick's head again, lift his chin again so I can kiss his lips, and say a silent "thank you."

Epilogue

Nick

8 MONTHS LATER

"We find the defendant guilty."

I'm sitting beside Aaron, our hands entwined so tightly I'm losing feeling in my fingers. But I don't care because the moment the verdict is read, he turns to me and collapses in tears on my shoulder. Despite the awkwardness of sitting on the hard benches in the courtroom gallery, I wrap him in my arms and let him sob. Around us, his family, Zack's friends, and several of my own are embracing, wiping tears from their eyes, and coming to terms with the fact that the man who killed Zack has just been convicted of the crime. It's an overwhelming moment, but my concern is Aaron and making sure he's all right.

A hand lands on my shoulder, and I look up to see Aaron's father. He pats me a couple of times, then nods and moves on to a cluster of Zack's friends. My heart warms that he knows I can take care of Aaron. And I will. I may not always be perfect, but I love the man I'm holding in my arms, and I will always be there for him if he needs me.

Kit is noticeably absent in the courtroom, but he had to be away from San Francisco for work this week. Aaron's told me he thinks Kit made up that excuse because he couldn't handle sitting through the trial, and maybe that's true. Kit's still in pretty bad shape, and no one seems to know what to do. My friends—bless them all—have seamlessly folded Aaron and Kit into our group, and our monthly get-togethers have moved into a rotating roster of our homes because no restaurant can hold us all without a lot of advance warning. Especially when Kit brings some of his and Zack's friends along as well. But all that social activity doesn't mean Kit isn't still noticeably flailing. It's given Aaron more than one sleepless night since we moved in together five months ago.

I glance around the courtroom as I place kisses on Aaron's head and rub my hands over his back. These people have become my family, I realize. My friends already were, but now that word embraces Aaron's friends and family as well. They've accepted and supported and, yes, loved me, and I am so grateful to be here for all of them on this momentous day.

The defendant, now a convicted murderer, rises from his seat when the bailiff and police officers move into position, ready to escort him back to his cell. In the gallery, we fall silent. Those of us who are still seated rise as they handcuff the man and then lead him out of the courtroom. Once he's out of our sight, we all breathe a collective sigh that is equal parts relief and regret.

While we wanted the conviction, while Aaron and his family deserved closure and Zack deserved justice, we have also talked about how this moment would feel if the jury agreed with the prosecution. I don't think anything could have prepared us for the enormity of it, the sheer overwhelm of emotions, and the bitter sorrow that two random people met up in a dark alley and only one walked away.

"We'd like to have everyone come over to our house this evening," Aaron's mother says. "It's not going to be a party. There's nothing really to celebrate here, but I think we all need to be with each other tonight."

There are murmurs and nods of agreement, but I turn to Aaron.

"How are you doing?"

He gives me a half-smile and shakes his head. "I don't know. I'm not sure it's sunk in yet that it's all over."

"The case at least," I say and melt a bit inside when Aaron's gaze turns soft like it always does when I show him how clearly I see him, how much I care about him.

"I love you," he says.

"I love you, too," I respond, leaning in for a quick kiss.

They clear us out of the courtroom, and our group spends a few more minutes in the hallway exchanging hugs. Helen reminds everyone about coming over that night. "Don't worry about bringing anything, we'll pick up some roasted chickens and sides on the way home," she says as a couple of Zack's friends make their good-byes.

Aaron and I hug her, hug Robert, then Ty and Roman wrap me up in their arms and tell me to take good care of Aaron.

"Of course," I say. "I am the world's best boyfriend. I've even got a mug at home to prove it." Which I actually do have because Aaron gave it to me for my birthday last month.

Ty shakes his head at me but doesn't give voice to his disbelief that I am one hundred percent on board with using the b-word—which makes me glad—but he still can't quite get over the fact that I'm in a monogamous and exclusive relationship. It's okay. I feel that way myself sometimes, but then I look at Aaron and know this is what I want. With him. For the rest of our lives.

Aaron and I say our goodbyes and head to the parking garage to reclaim his car and go home. Even though it's only one in the afternoon, I'm exhausted, so I can't imagine how Aaron's feeling. I offer to drive, and he gratefully hands over the keys.

As I drive through the city to Noe Valley, Aaron plays with the hair on the back of my neck. I can tell he's drifting off when his hand stills. I hate to wake him as I pull into our garage, but we're home, and we both need to reclaim some of the sleep we lost last night worrying about jury deliberations going into a second day.

"Come on, sleepyhead," I say as I release his seatbelt. I lay a soft kiss on his lips. "Time to get some real sleep."

We're met at the garage door by a wiggling ball of fluff in the form of our Soft-Coated Wheaton Terrier, Sophia. She's nine months old, adorable, and totally Aaron's dog. Case in point, she ignores me completely in favor of greeting Aaron with soft woofles, her short tail wagging a mile a minute. I'd be jealous except that when she's done greeting him, she comes over to me. I squat down so she can give me kisses.

"I'll walk her," I say looking up at Aaron. "You go take a shower and get in bed."

"Sounds good," he says and heads upstairs.

I collect Sophia's leash and take her for a short walk around the block. By the time I'm back, Aaron is sound asleep in our bed. It gives me a moment to take him in. This incredible man who came into my life in the oddest of ways has become the center of it. I'm pretty sure there will be a ring soon and then a wedding. I know for a fact that there's already a pool for who's going to pop the question as well as when it will happen because Sash let it slip about a month ago.

At the time, it freaked me out, but now, as I think about all the people who were at the courthouse and envision them watching Aaron and me exchange vows, I realize it's what I want. I want this man to be my husband. Now, it's just a matter of figuring out when to ask him. And completely misleading my friends about what I'm planning.

THE END

Power of Attorney, Book Three in the Legal Briefs Novella Series, brings you the story of Roman and the guy who wandered into his bookstore in chapter five. It will be available in the summer of 2026, but you can get a sneak peek at the first chapter here:

Also by

Marie Sinclair

Because my list of titles is always growing, I invite you to check out my current list of books here:

All my titles are available on Amazon and in KU

I love hearing from my readers. If you'd like to join my newsletter (and get a free novella) or follow me on social media, I invite you to visit my one-stop shop link to all that and more:

ABOUT THE AUTHOR

Marie Sinclair is a queer, agender (pronouns they/them) writer who lives in San Francisco. They were a finalist for the 2023 Lambda Literary Award in Gay Romance, received an IPPY Gold Medal for Best Romance Ebook in 2024, and was awarded first place in the 2025 Writer's Digest Self-Published Book Award for Genre Fiction.

Their focus is on contemporary romance with characters and stories that will take you on an emotional journey to a hard-won HEA. As a member of the LGBTQ+ community, Marie believes in rooting their stories in the real world of queer culture and showing how love can survive even in challenging times. The power of romance lies in hope, and that is what Marie offers in all their books.

Made in the USA
Coppell, TX
16 April 2026

75592333R10079